PENGUIN BOOKS

THE NARROWING STREAM

John Mortimer is a former barrister and the author of many novels, stage and television plays, film scripts, and plays for radio, including six plays on the life of Shakespeare, and the Rumpole plays, which won him the British Academy Writer of the Year Award. He has also translated Feydeau for the National Theatre and Johann Strauss's *Die Fledermaus* for the Royal Opera House, now available from Viking, and adapted *Brideshead Revisited* for television.

Six of Mortimer's books of Rumpole stories (*Rumpole of the Bailey, The Trials of Rumpole, Rumpole's Return, Rumpole for the Defense, Rumpole and the Golden Thread,* and *Rumple's Last Case*), all available from Penguin, have been collected into two volumes, *The First Rumpole Omnibus* and *The Second Rumpole Omnibus*. Penguin also publishes *Rumpole and the Age of Miracles,* the seventh Rumpole book; *In Character* and *Character Parts,* interviews with some of the most prominent men and women of our time; *Clinging to the Wreckage,* his celebrated autobiography, which won the 1982 *Yorkshire Post* Book of the Year Award; and a volume of plays including *A Voyage Round My Father*. His best-selling novel, *Paradise Postponed,* published in Viking and Penguin, was a much-acclaimed television series in 1986. The sequel, *Titmuss Regained,* was published by Viking in 1990, as was the eighth collection of Rumpole stories, *Rumpole à la Carte*. Another recent novel, *Summer's Lease* (Viking, 1988), was published in Penguin in 1989. His early novels, which are also now available from Penguin, include *Charade,* first published here in 1986, and *Like Men Betrayed,* originally published in 1954 and reissued in the U.S. by Viking in 1989. *The Narrowing Stream* was first published in England in 1954.

THE
NARROWING
STREAM

JOHN MORTIMER

PENGUIN BOOKS

For Penelope

PENGUIN BOOKS
Published by the Penguin Group
Viking Penguin, a division of Penguin Books USA Inc.,
375 Hudson Street, New York, New York 10014, U.S.A.
Penguin Books Ltd, 27 Wrights Lane,
London W8 5TZ, England
Penguin Books Australia Ltd, Ringwood,
Victoria, Australia
Penguin Books Canada Ltd, 2801 John Street,
Markham, Ontario, Canada L3R 1B4
Penguin Books (N.Z.) Ltd, 182–190 Wairau Road,
Auckland 10, New Zealand

Penguin Books Ltd, Registered Offices:
Harmondsworth, Middlesex, England

First published in the United States of America by
Viking Penguin, a division of Penguin Books USA Inc., 1989
Published in Penguin Books 1990

1   3   5   7   9   10   8   6   4   2

LIBRARY OF CONGRESS CATALOGING IN PUBLICATION DATA
Mortimer, John Clifford, 1923–
The narrowing stream/John Mortimer.
p.   cm.
Originally published: Avanpress, 1954.
ISBN 0 14 01.4421 8
I. Title.
PR6025.O7552N37   1990
823'.914 — dc20   90–38711

Printed in the United States of America

THE
NARROWING
STREAM

THE boy, white and tense as a soldier going into battle, let himself into the water. His sister, still comfortably dressed, watched him and fed the swans. The boy liked to punish himself; occasionally he tied himself up or purposely brushed his knee against a stinging nettle. He was ten. So he swam before breakfast.

The river, black and mysterious, rose up to meet him and closed over his head. He came up paddling wildly, his hair flattened down like a mongrel dog. Then he started a breast stroke, his pale arms and legs waving above the green weeds.

'Where are you going?' the girl asked him with amusement. The boy didn't answer, pretending to be too grand to speak. In fact, he had no breath and his mouth was full of river.

The red brick house had a lawn that stretched down to the river and two boathouses. One of the boathouses his father used; the other was empty. The boy was going to swim to the empty boathouse because it frightened him so much.

They had a big house because of the three children and because his father was doing all right. It was an ugly house with too many passages and a glass porch and it looked as if it had once been a vicarage. In fact, it had once been used to house a number of Catholic priests and, in an excess of faith, a statue of St Anthony had been put in a niche above the empty, sham Gothic boathouse. This feminine, benedictory saint of the drowning, raising his fingers above the door, added to the boy's fear. He had once heard his father talk about a mortuary by the Seine and he at once thought of this boathouse, with a shelving platform round the inside for the bodies and no floor except the black water and a saint over the entrance to help you to drown in holiness.

He had lost sight of his sister. There was a curious thin sound over the water. It was the boy singing to keep his spirits up.

He was opposite the entrance now. It rose above him square and dark, with a clump of rushes on one side. The water in the boathouse was stiller and more brackish than the water outside, and the confined space collected the flotsam of the river. Old cigarette cartons, a bottle, a piece of driftwood, floated on its surface so that it looked solid and neglected, like an unswept floor. At the entrance the boy stopped swimming and moved his arms and legs to keep himself afloat sitting in the water.

'Just look in, Sam,' he said to himself. 'Just look in, and then you can go home.' Then he changed to a rapid narrative in which he spoke of himself in the third person. '*Slowly and silently the intrepid Maximillian swam up to the lowered portcullis. His arms made no sound cleaving the dark water. The two guards were asleep, their halberds piled against the wall.*' He rolled over on to his stomach in the water and swam towards the entrance.

Inside the boathouse it was shallow enough for him to stand and he did so, the mud oozing between his toes. He said 'Boom', but rather quietly, afraid to taunt the echo in earnest. He looked round and everything was the same. The leaky, useless punt was on the platform on the left-hand side. On the right was a pile of old motor tyres and empty paraffin drums. There were sacks on the platform beside him; only, possibly, one more than usual.

It was when he crouched down into the water to swim out that he saw the man's face.

IT was not noticed by the children that their mother was beautiful. They had breakfast in the kitchen and she walked round them wearing a light cotton dress, her body still firm and desirable, her face clean of make-up but, like the face of a statue from which the paint has been washed away, with traces of pinkness over the lips and blue shadow above the eyes. She walked with her eyes a little closed, as if the sun were always in them, and her hair, which also had the appearance of having been polished by the sun, was caught up over the nape of her neck in a way which was never secure. She hadn't laid a place for herself at breakfast, but she drank a cup of coffee standing up.

Why, Swinton thought, can't she sit down? It was as if having children made life full of continual crises, like a perpetual air-raid when the victims have to snatch what refreshment they can between the alerts. They had been married a long time so that he, too, only vaguely noticed the calmness of the way she stood, the beauty of her face and figure.

Swinton went on putting on his collar, a thing he was always left to do with one hand while he tried to eat his breakfast with the other. With his collarless striped shirt he looked, for a moment, like a middle-aged but astute carpenter. It was a moment during which his wife felt an odd passion for him, a passion which flickered out when she realized that he was going to read aloud, as he always did at breakfast, one of the advertisements on the front of the paper folded against the coffee pot.

' "Young man, university degree, seeks post with intelligent, anti-social employer. Pref. millionaire." Really, what answers can he hope to get?'

Because we're not young, and have no need to advertise, Julia Swinton thought, we shouldn't laugh. Anyway, perhaps he doesn't want any answers.

The three children stared at their father, unsmiling. Susan, his eldest daughter, liked him least when he was putting his collar on. Few of the nicer girls at her school, she felt, had fathers who put their collars on at breakfast.

'Look out,' his younger daughter, Clara, said. 'You'll get your tie in the milk.'

At last he was dressed, turned from a carpenter to a business man, a business man with a small factory on the outskirts of London, who paid his workmen in person, and turned out furniture too well to make any extraordinary profit. When he was dressed and respectable, Susan sighed with resignation and relief.

Julia looked at him. Without his collar his head and neck had looked unexpectedly defenceless, as they did when he was asleep. She saw, with a shock, that even the little clump of hairs under his jawbone, the inch that was in shadow when he stood in front of the bathroom mirror and that he missed when he was shaving, was quite grey. Soon, she thought, he will be almost old. Not that it mattered; he had always had the sort of face that was inappropriate on a young man and, although she had first fallen in love with him for a certain blunt maturity in his features, it had taken time, almost until the present, for him to catch up with the lines and tolerant character of his face. For a moment, with the neck naked, the face was abstract and timeless, like the worn, bitten face on a coin or the unattached head on a passport, and then her husband was civilized, in a white collar and a tie that was just too consciously chosen for that of a civil servant and just too expensive for that of a painter. He's got his collar and tie on, Julia thought, ready to go away, and when he's here somehow or another we never get a chance to talk or be together. And yet, surely, they were still in love.

It was another day and he was looking at them, at his wife and children, with the vague look of oppression with which he looked at accounts, bank statements, market quotations. The look that he had when he saw a new design for something he thought beautiful and practicable Julia now saw on him rarely, and for a moment she resented his weary complacency at getting up, tying his tie at breakfast, catching his train. She had an unreasoned impulse to ask him to stay at home, to go out with them on the river, to make the day different and fill it, for both of them, with sudden and unexpected pleasure. She almost suggested it as the children looked at them both unblinking, their jaws working on their breakfast. You could tell who the children were because they had their names painted on their cups; Susan, Clara and Sam, the little boy.

But then Swinton started to read them another advertisement and the doorbell rang. Clara ran out and came back with a bill from the laundry and a folder from a firm of timber merchants.

Susan said: 'No letters for me?'

Clara gave her the bright folder on the cover of which was a photograph of a large and modern sawmill.

'Idiot. I mean no letter from Wilkins?'

'When you grow up,' Swinton said, 'you'll know it's a great relief not to get letters.'

'Wilkins would hardly write the day she's coming to stay, would she, darling? She is coming to stay today, isn't she?'

'Of course she is.'

'What the hell,' Swinton asked, 'is Wilkins?'

'Everyone told you last night. Susan's best friend from school.'

'Hasn't she got a Christian name?'

'Actually, she has,' Susan said coldly, 'but at school one doesn't use them.'

'I'm late. You'd better take me to the station. I suppose you'll need the car for this Timpkins.'

Susan sighed, her eyes turned upwards, as if in silent, hopeless prayer. Julia was smiling, conciliatory.

'Get her name right, darling, at that age they're touchy about that sort of thing. Shall I meet your train this evening?'

'I don't know. I can't honestly tell when I'll be back.'

'Oh.' She looked at him. He was standing up now and putting on his coat, the cloth stretched tightly across his broad shoulders, his head bent and turned away from her. She was puzzled for a moment at his vagueness, she couldn't understand why the evening suddenly seemed a long time away, uncertain, difficult to forecast.

'I'll meet you if you want. Perhaps you could telephone.'

'Perhaps . . .' The big man was looking down at Sam as if he had noticed him for the first time. The boy was also silent and oppressed, as like his father as a small, subtle and only moderately cruel caricature.

'You haven't had any breakfast,' Swinton said.

'I'm not hungry.'

'It's swimming,' Clara said. 'It makes him sick.'

'What's the matter, Sam?' Swinton spoke quietly, and the boy looked down at his plate.

'Nothing at all.'

There was a silence all round the table and for the first time the day was different from the other mornings in the Swintons' lives. There was no time to investigate the silence which was momentary, like the silence which is said to fall when a stranger steps on a future grave.

'All right. Let's go to the station. Are you all ready?'

Julia said: 'Right away. Could I have a cigarette?'

Swinton slapped his pockets automatically and shook his head. 'I've left my case somewhere.'

'Shall I look upstairs?' Clara got up suddenly, unexpectedly helpful.

'Don't bother. I'll find it this evening. Coming, Susan?'

'Not me,' Susan shook her head wearily. 'I've got to put some flowers in Wilkins's room.'

'Does she like flowers?'

'As a matter of fact, they bore her,' Susan sighed. 'Only she'd probably notice if they weren't there.'

AS they walked up the platform, Julia felt how hot and still the day was going to be. The train stood panting as if it were never going to move, a small, cumbersome, dirty train retching and belching smoke among the sweet peas and wallflowers of the country station. The children wandered down the platform in front of her, staggering with the frightful lassitude of childhood. And then Sam ran back to her and held her by the wrist, his head pressed against her thigh. Automatically she put her hand on his hair. She stood like that, watching her husband climb into the train, settle himself in a corner seat. Already, she felt, he was remote from her, strange and removed from the world of beds and children, gone into his own life where she had no part and which she didn't understand. She saw him fingering his paper, she thought that he was looking forward to the moment when he would be able to read it, when he had left her behind.

A whistle blew. The guard, with his yellowing-white moustache and enormous buttonhole, swung himself on to the end of the train. Swinton closed the door as the train began to move. Illogically, Julia thought: I really don't know anything about him, I have no idea what he's going to do all day. As the train wheels ground into motion she heard Sam say something. He hadn't spoken since breakfast.

'I don't want to go back,' he said.

She turned down to speak to him, too late to wave Swinton goodbye. 'Where, Sam? You don't want to go back where?'

'Home. To the boathouse. I think there's someone there.'

'Goodbye!' Swinton was standing up at the window, waving his paper.

Julia felt a moment of panic. She wanted to run beside the train, to tell him what Sam had said. But both the children were holding on to her now, Clara jumping and waving, Sam silent, waving slowly. She stood still and the train had gone. They were the only people on the platform.

When they were alone she bent over Sam. 'What did you say, Sam, about the boathouse?'

He let go her hand, looked at the ground. 'Nothing. Nothing, really. It was only part of my game.'

There was a long thundering behind them as a porter pulled up a truck of mail bags. The noise brought Julia back to reality. There was no cause for alarm, Sam's games were notoriously eccentric.

'Your game,' Clara said, jumping over the shadow of a long defunct chocolate machine, 'is quite barmy.'

As they got back into the car, Sam went on telling himself, '*Although they questioned him for hours his lips were sealed. He could not reveal the hiding place of his king.*'

Driving back slowly through the town, stopping as farmers' wives, their enormous buttocks uneasily poised over gaunt bicycles, swayed in front of the windscreen, slowing down to allow a cluster of children sucking ice-cream to cross the road in front of Woolworth's, Julia felt relaxed, at ease. In point of fact, there was going to be nothing wrong with the day apart from Susan's temperament and the dreaded arrival of Wilkins. Before lunch she could sit in the garden and pod the beans, after it she could cut herself out a new dress. Remote, as at the end of a long and narrowing road, lay the moment of the day when she would sit opposite her husband by the empty fireplace and tell him that Wilkins was worse, oh, infinitely worse, than any of them had imagined.

She liked driving the car and was better at it than Swinton would ever admit. She turned deftly down the side street at the end of the town, and over the bridge, then she drove down the long lane with a high hedge on each side that led down to the river and the house. Clara was singing in the back. Sam was silent.

The car, she thought, was like them, a long, black, respectable car but full of small signs of the good times they had had, from the battered G.B. plate on the back to the pigeonhole in front of the passenger's seat which still smelt of the bottle of Chanel she had taken with her through France. Uneasily, like contraband in the boot, rolled the beer bottles which she'd have to take back to the pub during the day, and on the floor in the back were the signs of the children she found curiously comforting, the outside of a comic, an empty bag of potato crisps and one gym shoe.

She parked in front of the garage and, as the children climbed out, she remembered again what had happened at the station. The sun was on the front of the house and on the garden and it looked peaceful, the red brick almost mellow, the doors and windows all open to let in the air. In the shadows of trees by the river she saw the roof of the old boathouse and she thought that when she had put her shopping away she would go down there to make sure Sam was talking non-sense.

She was stopped, however, by the visitors she found in the sitting-room.

'*Blood will have Blood*,' the elderly woman said who stood in the doorway. She was a little, bent woman with a black crocheted cap and a pale blue eye-shade. She wore now, as in most weathers, a faded Burberry and tennis shoes. She had a long, spade-shaped face, liberally dusted with dead-white powder. She was Miss Lorwood. The man by the bookcase was her brother Perkin. They had come, as usual, to borrow books.

The Lorwoods' bungalow was nearer to the water than the Swintons' house. They had an old dinghy which they kept in the garden and used for growing nasturtiums in. Although elderly and retired, filling in tedious days by reading detective stories and cooking on paraffin, they always had a remotely nautical appearance. Perkin in particular, apart from tennis shoes, wore very shrunk white flannel trousers with most of the buttons undone. In his small, withered hand he carried a yachting cap.

'*Blood will have Blood,*' Miss Lorwood repeated. 'It's your husband's. I've read it.'

Julia took it automatically. 'He buys these things on stations,' she said. 'I can't think why.'

Perkin was looking out of the window. Over the bean-posts at the end of the garden the asbestos roof of his bungalow was visible. 'Making a good deal of smoke, isn't it, our oven this morning?'

'He's always seeing things out of windows,' his sister told Julia. 'He looks out of ours or into other people's most of the time.'

Nervously, Perkin contemplated the dark, votive cloud issuing from above his kitchen.

'All the same, my dear, there's something about that joint, I dare swear, that's not altogether Bristol fashion.'

'It must be difficult,' Julia said, 'cut off down there with no real facilities.'

'Not a scrap of it.' Perkin turned round, suddenly excited. 'Perfectly good facilities. Just bury it at the bottom of the garden. Laughably easy job. Why, if you got a fatigue like that in the army you'd laugh at it, simply laugh!'

'He does talk a lot,' his sister whispered to Julia, 'since he's got so deaf.'

'Or if it's before six in the morning – well, it just goes in the river. By gummy, look at that smoke.'

'Come away from the window,' his sister suddenly shouted. 'You're always peering out at something!'

'Do you want another book?' Julia waved vaguely at the shelves. It was still all right, a hot day and a visit from the Lorwoods, which was a nuisance when she had such a lot to do. She reminded herself to stop Sam swimming in the river. Somewhere about, surely, there would be a safe indoor swimming bath with chlorine in the water.

'Have you a nice one? I like a plain murder. Perkin had one last week from the library, a horrible long thing about a courtesan in the time of Marie Antoinette. I can't think why he should want to read about all that diving in and out of bed with people. I simply can't see what it holds for him,' Miss Lorwood muttered to herself as she wandered along the shelves. Her brother detached himself from the window. Julia lit a cigarette, wondering how long they could possibly stay.

'I've been reading a bit of history lately. French history, you know. Instructive sort of stuff.'

'We've got Carlyle's *French Revolution*.' Julia heard herself speaking from a long way off. 'Susan won it as a prize at school.'

'Have you, by gum?' Perkin spoke with the awe with which people hear that their neighbours have just contracted a fatal disease. He backed away from the solemn, leather-bound book and went back to the window. 'I say, look at your young shaver. Curious form of ritual dance, that. Anyone who didn't know your good selves would have suspected Arab blood.'

'He's not dancing.' Julia joined him at the window. 'He's fighting.'

'Really?' Miss Lorwood tiptoed up beside them. 'And who's he fighting now?'

'No one.' Julia suddenly felt hopelessly apologetic. 'He just does it. From time to time.'

The heat was shimmering over the lawn and on it Sam was capering, a short garden stake in one hand, the other raised behind him in the position adopted by masters of the epée and foil. One wrist was bandaged with his handkerchief, a mere scratch caused by the sabre of Count Von Blunitz, traitor and anti-Royalist adventurer. Luckily, it was a flesh wound. It had missed the artery. A vicious attack from the Count forced him down to one knee, he was tired and losing a devilish lot of blood. All the same, he rallied and beat his enemy back to the shrubbery. Now he was advancing remorselessly towards the old boat-house; there was cover there, shelter from the bullets of Von Blunitz's men, hired Bavarian lackeys who were skulking now, without doubt, in the shadows of the monkey-puzzle tree.

Perkin held back the curtain with one hand as he gazed out. 'Does it often happen like that?' he asked. 'Or only in the hotter weather?'

The two old people with Julia between them had been watching the performance of Sam's, fascinated. Now Miss Lorwood pulled them all together. 'You must stop him, Mrs Swinton,' she said, 'peeping out. He says he sees the most ridiculous things. This morning he almost persuaded me not to come and return the book. He said he thought you had a visitor staying.'

'A visitor?' Julia moved back into the room. 'We shall have, later today. A girl. A friend of Susan's.'

'No, this wasn't a girl, Mrs Swinton. A man. Perkin thought he saw him last night, by your old boathouse.'

Julia saw their faces in front of the lawn. The lawn was empty and hot. Sam had gone. In the next minute she found herself running over the soft grass; it seemed to take her a very long time, like running in a dream.

Perkin was still at the window, watching.

'Strange family,' he said. 'Arab blood somewhere, without a doubt.'

WHEN Sam had fought his way into the trees by the boathouse he stood still. He became himself again, and afraid. He stood still so as not to make a noise. Around him were the big, dusty, ugly leaves of laurels and rhododendrons, dark green and dusty and smelling stale and bitter. There was a rustling among them and a big cat came out, the Lorwoods' cat from next door, a bloated animal with a coat like the faded furs Sam had seen round the necks of old women he hated. The cat had the same pointed, ferrety face as the faces of furs looking round the red, bloated necks of old women. Sam moved his leg so as not to be touched by it.

When the cat had gone he started to walk towards the door of the boathouse; it had a narrow door on the landward side fixed with a piece of string in place of the broken padlock. He was going to untie the string and look inside. It wasn't because he wanted to do this but because he had to. He knew that the first step he took would

start something that had to end by his untying the
string and looking into the old boathouse. It was
like finding a dead rat in the path on his way to
school. He hated seeing it but he knew that he
would have to come back from school by the
same path and that when he passed the place again
he would have to look.

His need to see this was stronger than his need
to see a rat.

Often, when he was lonely, he thought of
finding, in this way, a friend. Sometimes he
thought it was going to be a dwarf-like creature
who would do exactly as he told it. Sometimes
that it would be an enormous, stupid and faithful
servant. His fear had gone and he had a longing,
an affection, for the face he had seen. He pulled
eagerly at the string, worrying the knot with his
nails and then with his teeth. In the end he loos-
ened it. He tugged at the door. It stuck at first and
then it flew open, he staggered back with it as if
there had been a sudden explosion in the boathouse and he had been knocked back by the blast.

'Sam!' His mother held him as he fell back. His
face was against hers, she was looking over his
shoulder. Their faces were oddly similar although
the boy was laughing and his mother afraid.
'Sam, what is it? What have you seen?'

Her voice echoed against the walls of the single
floorless room. There was no one there.

IT was useless to ask Sam anything more. He had shut up suddenly like a clam and when she spoke to him he looked at the ground and kicked a little stone. The Lorwoods might tell her something, and as quickly as she could Julia got back to the house. She brought Sam with her, dragging him by the hand so as not to let him out of her sight.

But when she got back to the sitting-room the Lorwoods had left. The room seemed stuffy and airless to her, and the things she liked, the long white bookcases, the porcelain Venus on the window-sill, the big modern picture over the mantel-piece, looked older and dirtier than she had thought. She left Sam standing resentfully in a patch of sunshine in the middle of the carpet and went to the door to call: 'Susan! Clara! Come here, will you?'

She was trembling, and there was panic in her voice. 'Clara! Clara, where are you?'

'Here. Haven't you got eyes?' The little, narrow girl uncoiled herself from where she had been lying, improbably, on the stairs, reading a book.

'Where's Susan?'

'Here, for heaven's sake.' Susan came out of the kitchen. In her hand was an old salmon and shrimp paste-pot which contained three corn-flowers in water.

When she had assembled them, Julia looked at them apologetically. She said: 'It must be time for Wilkins's train.'

'I was thinking that,' Susan said. 'These are for her dressing-table.'

'Lovely, darling.' She sat down on the arm of a chair, found a cigarette. 'She'll love them.'

'I'll go and put them upstairs.'

'No. No, don't bother. Put them on the book-case. I'll take them up later.'

She wanted to keep them all together until they left the house. And yet it was absurd. In some way or other the day would have to go on. They would come back, get the lunch; the children would play, running through the bedrooms to change their clothes, they were always either too hot or too cold. If she wanted a search made of the place she'd better tell someone. She could think more clearly when they were out of the house. Perhaps she would find someone to consult, perhaps, in the end, the right thing was to tell the police.

They arrived at the station far too early for the train from London, so anxious had she been to get them all away from the house. There was nothing for the children to do but run up and down the station entrance and jump on the weighing-machine, or beg her for pennies for comics. Susan sat aloof, practising the expression of bored disgust which she kept for her best friends.

Outside the station standing in the sun and reading the first edition of the *Evening Standard* was a tall, heavy man in blue shorts whose narrowing, strangely white legs ended, somehow inappropriately, in little, almost feminine sandals. So detached seemed his feet from his large, spotty face, iron-grey hair and heavy horned-rimmed spectacles that he had the appearance of one of those drawings which children pass to each other folded, adding legs, knees and feet in turn and ignorant of what has gone before, to be opened at the end with shrieks of laughter. Finally, in such games a name and even an occupation is added. In this case they would not have detracted from the fun. It was Campbell, who took part in parlour games over the wireless, on holiday for a fortnight in his launch by the river, a launch that the Swintons had found moored inconveniently close to their house.

'Yippee.' Campbell spoke in a very deep voice with a reassuringly cultivated accent, acquired during his early days as a dealer in second-hand cars. 'How's glamour this morning?'

Julia smiled at him faintly, feeling idiotic.

'Packing the kids off on the next train? How superlatively right.'

'As a matter of fact, no. Another one's coming.'

'Male or female created he them?'

'Female, about sixteen.'

Campbell made an extraordinary noise, apparently symbolic of male desire, but in fact exactly like the final disappearance of bath water. 'More glamour?'

'I shouldn't think so.'

'Pity. Big pity, in fact. I'm having nearly all the river in for drinks tonight. You and your Lord and Master will come, of course?'

'I don't know what time my husband will be back – we're going to be awfully tied up with the children.' She made the excuses automatically, knowing how Swinton loathed the man. In fact, the invitation gave her a sudden pleasure at the thought of the lonely day ending, of Swinton being with her again.

'Do come. Big ginnies for us, big tomato juices for the teenage glamour. Mix a drop of gin in their tomato juice and wow, anything can happen.'

Captivated by the thought of gin in Wilkins's tomato juice, Julia softened. 'Perhaps,' she said. 'We'll see if we can get away.'

'Do that very thing. Besides, everyone will be talking. I want to hear the lowdown on Molly.'

'Molly?'

'Molly Paneth. You've met her in the bars round here, haven't you? Medium-sized blonde with all the fixings.'

Far down the line a puff of smoke was visible. Sam and Clara were clinging to the grille at the entrance to the platform like mothers whose sons are about to return from long periods as prisoners of war. Susan sighed and averted her head. 'Will she have a blue hat on?' Clara was asking. 'Will her cat be coming with her?'

'I think you told me,' Julia said. 'Didn't she have the island houseboat?'

'Ramshackle place. But you must have seen her. Calling her a blonde I may have given you the wrong idea. I mean she wasn't one of those blondes out of a bottle. She was the real thing. Small, you know, but extraordinary. If you saw her once you couldn't forget her.'

He edged towards her, as if anxious to make her admit the fascination of a girl she had never seen.

'No. I'm sure not. I think you told us about her. Wasn't she an actress?'

Campbell nodded eagerly, as if encouraged by her question.

'By way of being one. Came down to learn a part. She wasn't so wonderful as an actress. We had her once on the programme, you know. But she didn't really tie in. Couldn't even spot what it was when I imitated a chicken.'

Susan moved hurriedly away from them as Campbell imitated one again, to show how easy it was to spot. As the chicken expired, he said: 'I thought there might be something about her in the evening paper.'

Julia was turning her head vaguely, watching the passengers coming out of the train. 'Why?' she asked. 'What did she do?'

'Got killed.'

She had been watching the first enthusiastic arrivals, men and girls starting their holidays who jumped off the running-board while the train was still moving to run round to the guard's van for their bicycles. Now she turned to where his face, big, sweating slightly, larger than life-size, seemed to grow and waver in front of her like a close-up in the cinema.

'What do you mean? Did she die?'

'Some sort of accident, apparently. I haven't a clue how it happened. Anyway, there's big excitement over by the island this morning.'

He had the paper up again and was turning the pages over, blowing his cheeks out thoughtfully.

'Poor Mol. A party girl in her way, too. Possibly at the time. That may have been it.'

'Mummy! Mummy!' Clara was shrieking from the barrier. 'She's arrived. We've seen her. She's getting out.'

There was nothing tangible to worry her, nothing to be afraid of. It wasn't that Sam had talked about a man in an empty boathouse and, farther down the river, a girl who had apparently been beautiful had died. There was only a feeling that the hot, silent endless day couldn't be spent alone with the children. She wanted the house filled with grown-up people, laughing, eating lunch, drinking gin. She wanted the silence broken, the vague mystery dispelled. She didn't want to be left alone.

'You must come over today,' she said. 'Come over to the house.'

The edge of the paper swung down like a horizon seen from a ship in a storm. Behind the thick glasses the eyes were moist, filled with gratitude.

'Come over today? Does that mean – I have a chance?'

Suddenly she remembered what she hoped to have been able to forget. The last party in the horrible little chromium and teak cabin of the launch, the smell of gin and sun oil, her eyes riveted to a bas-relief of a galleon done in china and hung on the wall. In a corner Swinton was making loudly pugnacious remarks about the wireless programmes to a girl in green trousers. On the sofa next to her Campbell was whispering: 'Any afternoon when he's in London. Please try and make it. I've waited so long for you. Tell me I've got a chance.'

'Mummy. This is Wilkins.' Susan had sidled up to her, staggering with her friend's case. Julia didn't look round, staring at the man in front of her.

'Not today, perhaps. It's a bit awkward. I'll give you a ring.'

All the children were round her now, standing in various attitudes of possession like some ancient guard which both traps and protects their ruler. Campbell folded up his paper, backing away.

'Fine,' he said. 'That's fine. You do that very thing.'

'Come on, Wilkins,' Susan said. 'This is our car.'

'No, really?' Wilkins said. 'How amusing.'

JULIA was being pulled on by the two younger children, towed like a sailing ship by two dirty, puffing tugs. She turned back her head, allowing Campbell a final view of her perfect, unsmiling features, of long hair caught at the nape of her neck, of her dress creasing as her breasts moved under it. He pushed his lips to whistle but at the sight of so many children his spirit failed and no sound emerged from him. Julia looked down on her visitor with some awe and apprehension. She expected her next remark to be: 'And is that your mother? How quaint.' She bundled them into the car, giving Wilkins the seat of honour beside her.

'I'll stop in the town,' Julia said, 'and see if I can find some strawberries for lunch.'

'If that's specially for me' – Wilkins was gazing out of the window – 'don't bother. I don't care for them, actually.'

She was a small, not unhandsome girl dressed as for the depths of winter in a tweed overcoat and a little round felt hat. She also wore gloves.

'Mummy,' Clara shouted from the back seat. 'When we get back can we all take Wilkins out in the punt? Can we take a picnic?'

'Perhaps she doesn't like punts.'

'Oh, I don't mind them' – Wilkins smiled tolerantly – 'provided I don't have to row.'

'Rowing a punt,' Sam said suddenly to no one, 'is barmy.'

Julia rebuked him half-heartedly and the conversation lapsed.

They were all in the car moving back towards the house. Alone like all women and children in the daytime when the men are away, Julia drove slowly, delaying their arrival. The day had again become a dream, a nightmare from which she hoped, sometime, to awake. A girl she couldn't have seen more than once in her life was dead, Sam worrying her about a face that he had probably imagined. There wasn't enough in it for her to do anything at all, but she drove slowly, stopping at the fruit shop by the crossroads even though Wilkins was above strawberries.

When she came back she had made up her mind to tell someone, to stop it all at once. She was vague, benevolent, female and unwilling to give trouble. All the same, the fear was driving her out of herself, fear like smoke which is used to dislodge a swarm of bees. She stood by the car helplessly for a moment, a chip of strawberries in her hand, the sticky, blood-red berries nestling on cabbage leaves, her arm turned to show the white inside with the blue vein at her wrist. She waited, and the children, who had been too exhausted to come with her into the shop, lowered at her from inside of the car.

She saw a policeman and started to speak. As she opened her mouth, he said: 'Is that your motor car?'

'Well, yes. Yes, it is.'

He drew a long, official breath. 'Surely it must have been clear to you from the presence of vehicles beside the opposite pavement that there was no parking on this side today?'

The children from inside the car saw her hands move, her lips smile apologetically. Graceful and rebuked she came back into the car and drove them home.

THE children wanted to show Wilkins the river as soon as they got home. The river was always there, all round them, but it couldn't wait. They had to get the punt out straight away, leaving Julia alone in the house.

A house on a river is different altogether from a house by the sea, and children by the river are differently, more lazily but more intensely occupied than children by the sea. About the water which flowed past their garden there was nothing violent or restless. The river was calm, and yet it had its own character and its own mystery. It was made, timelessly, for pleasure.

The river was pleasure; nothing serious navigated it, the houses on its islands were too prone to be flooded to be lived in permanently, purposefully, all the year round. The fish in it were too small to be eaten, almost too small to be caught. It was not fun, as the crowds might have thought, passing over it too fast in steamers on Bank Holidays, playing concertinas and drinking bottled beer round the clock; it had its moments of sourness, of treachery and of death. Yet in all these moments the pleasure was there, so that the dance music, the kisses, the champagne corks of fifty years ago still echoed under the trees. The newest chromium-fitted launch, nosing its way along the side of the stream, disturbed with its wash the broken hulk of a derelict house-boat, scene of some scandalous and forgotten love-affair.

Past the Swintons' house the river widened, becoming too wide for the children to swim. The end of the town was on one bank with its concrete towpath and the yew hedges and flagpole at the end of the bowling green. There was something urban and sad about that bank, the men fishing there wore trouser clips and trilby hats; the love-making was carried on on the hard benches of the Borough Council. Far away on the opposite bank the wooded hills climbed to a plateau of cornfields and a red-brick church tower. On the riverside were the bungalows of those whose prosperity showed itself by owning launches and Alsatian dogs. Here was the best market for gin and bronze statuettes and television, where the men wore blue blazers and old school ties which only just failed to carry conviction and the women continued to an inappropriate age the practice of wearing shorts.

Between the two banks were a succession of islands. Some of them were small, only large enough for nettles and trees and the nest of the aloof, predatory family of swans who stretched their necks and hissed at Sam as he floated by, scaring him badly. Others were larger, and by them, forty years ago, had been moored the houseboats, beautiful white erections of wood and wrought iron, with inadequate bedrooms and no mobility at all. These houseboats had by no means all been built to the same pattern, but had allowed architectural fantasy, some castellated to look like the barge from which King Arthur might have answered slowly in a pre-Raphaelite painting, some with Egyptian motives suggesting Cleopatra's progress across the back of the stage at an Edwardian theatre. One by one, as age and the river worked on them, they had sunk or deteriorated. One or two had had their remnants dragged ashore, corrugated iron had added a scullery or an outside lavatory, and the family of a porter from the local station now lived painfully in the shell of a boat where a Captain of Hussars had once upset the baccarat table and, as a forfeit, had the ends of his moustache burned by a royal cigar.

The days of the houseboats were over, dead as the butlers who had once rowed over to them with hot rolls and the morning papers. The country house on the bank away from the town was shuttered and closed, and its own island a mass of weeds. On this particular island a Georgian owner had built a temple of love in which, under a miniature dome, an Italian Venus stood and sheltered her private parts with cold, stone hands. It was to this island that the last of the houseboats was moored, a small, frivolous

Noah's Ark, with wrought-iron railings on the roof and weeds in the hanging baskets which should have contained geraniums. The house-boat, like the temple itself, showed signs of neglect, it needed painting and it leaked. It belonged to a local boatman and he let it out in the summer to people who didn't care too much about the leaks or the paint, women who painted pictures or actresses like Molly Paneth.

Because of her, and because of the stone statue, it was still an amorous island, having about it a mystery that the children found strange and hos-tile. The tangle of ground ivy and convolvulus left patches of grass, thick and spongy and well shadowed by trees, which had long been the resort of lovers. About the houseboat and the island there had been a quiet, secret activity, unlike the straightforward parties with barrels of beer and young men from Cambridge, which had taken place in the bungalows on the mainland. Here the gramophone records had been of slow, enormous negresses murmuring sounds of deep tragedy or of German blondes whose throats seemed constricted with desire. The visitors came in couples, they stayed only a short time and were ever changing, so that as soon as the interested spectators on the mainland had one luxuriant girl focused in their binoculars she was gone, replaced by another. No one could make out, from the inappropriate times the parties on the houseboat were seen eating, what meals they had, some-times long after teatime they would give every appearance of being just about to sit down to lunch. At night the gramophone records would sound across the water, there would be a glimmer of white shirts and dresses on the roof of the houseboat as the couples danced in the dark.

Opposite the island, but a little way down the river, the municipality had built a bathing place with springboards, a water chute and cabins for changing in, where the people of the town could bathe in decency and where, almost alone on that stretch of the river, it was impossible to make love.

Now the island itself was quiet, a police launch was moored beside the houseboat and two men in peaked caps were playing cards in the cabin at the back. Nevertheless, the atmosphere remained.

'The statue island,' Clara said. 'Let's land.'

The two girls in the middle of the punt looked up, and the Venus, heavy lidded and stone-eyed, returned their gaze. Susan thought, if I could stop eating bread altogether, never again any more bread, then I might have a waist that went in like that. Wilkins pressed her lips together, the Venus regarded her, as it were, despairingly.

'Come on,' Clara said. 'I like it. Paddle us in, Sam.'

Sam stopped paddling and stared at the island. Once a master at his school had said to him: 'Nature – you should show more interest in Nature. You live by the river. Get up early one morning and try and spot how many different sorts of water fowl you can see.' He had taken the

punt and got on to the island, then, because he
was curious, he had stood on his toes to look
through the windows of the houseboat and had
seen a girl with no clothes on at all, boiling a kettle
on a paraffin stove. He thought she had little
blond hairs all down her spine like an animal.

'No,' he said. 'No, I won't. I don't like it.'

A man from the police launch got up and
shouted at them.

'Get away, you kids. Keep away from here.'

'We'll go on,' Sam said. 'On past the lock.'

Clara said: 'There's no time before lunch.'

'Yes, there is. Plenty of time.'

Sam was having to paddle the punt alone. He
sat at the end and jabbed the paddle viciously into
the water. There was a cloud of midges round his
head and when he felt the water it was hot, like
bath water. Susan and Wilkins trailed their hands
in the river. Clara lay on the deck, spreadeagled
in the sun, now and then waving her legs in the
air and rocking the punt. They were all, in Sam's
view, making it as difficult for him as possible.
He strained his thin arms and the mass of female,
adolescent flesh moved slowly over the weeds,
under the willows.

'*A grim smile twisting his lips, making his white teeth
shine in the mass of black beard, the Captain looked down
on the groaning mass of human misery between decks.
The sun shone on black backs, they were women mostly,
large, fat, oily girls for the slave markets of Demerara.
"What's their future?" the first mate asked him. "The
lucky ones," he said, "will die."* '

WHEN she was alone Julia felt better. She opened all the doors in the house and turned on the wireless so that the warm, treacly sound of a cinema organ surged between the rooms. She looked at the meat in the oven and put the vegetables on to boil and then she walked into the sitting-room to get herself a cigarette. For a while she stood still, watching the river at the end of the garden. The sun was shining and it was very still; hardly any boats came up this part of the river, which was a backwater off the main stream. It was going to be a long time, half an hour, three-quarters of an hour, before lunch was ready. She was going to get another meal in a long line of meals she had got, by which, as it now seemed to her miraculously, she had managed to keep the children alive, to put flesh on them and to make them grow. The time was empty, aimless, convenient for thought.

Watching the river she put her hands on her hips, pulled in her stomach and pushed out her breasts. Then she walked slowly across the room, her legs stiff, her body swaying, an absurd, exaggerated walk like the entrance of a principal boy in a pantomime. Would it have been good for her, she wondered, to have been a principal boy? Or a bus conductress, or a female pilot, or a great tragedienne? As she passed by her husband's desk she picked up a paperknife, a short silver knife with a handle made from an otter's paw hunted by Swinton's father; lifting it at arm's length she pointed it towards her breast. Then she saw herself in the mirror, graceful and dramatic, a talent wasted.

She put down the knife and crossed over to the mirror, pulled down her lip with her finger and began to examine her teeth. Then she put her hands on her hips again and smiled, a sudden, catlike grin. Being alone she forgot it was her home, her children on the river, her potatoes on the stove; she felt solitary, isolated, a stranger. Ordinarily, she thought, most of the day was a sort of death for her; she waited for the moment when Swinton came home to begin something, to live, and then when he came he was sleepy and silent and the best of the day was a sleepy death again in bed.

All the same, it was, at most times, lonely. She was left between the children, engrossed in their secret world, and Swinton equally engrossed and away from her at the other end of a railway line. It would have been better, no doubt – now she pushed her hands down her thighs, straightening her dress – it would have been better never to have married, to have had a succession of lovers each younger than the last, to have worn, after the age of thirty, a collection of mysterious hats. It would have been better but not her, not Julia Swinton, and she sighed, letting the sound out heavily into the still room. Her life was made for her, fixed, now too late for a change.

And then her sigh, cut short before the end was reached, stopped, and she held her breath. She knew that she was being watched.

It was by no one inside the room, the door was shut behind her and the furniture was too low for any concealment. The big windows were open, the garden silent, but she knew that if she turned away from the mirror she would see someone in the garden watching her.

The terror cut into her, clean and cold like very cold water rising to cover a bather. At the same time it woke her, she felt herself tingling. It was a sharp relief after the vague uneasiness of the morning. She felt as if she had found something she had been looking for, now that she had found something to fear.

But she didn't look towards the garden. She turned her head to the door and walked slowly towards it, stiff inside with fear, resisting the temptation to run. When she got into the passage she shut the door behind her, shutting away the windows that looked out on to the garden.

She walked into the kitchen and slowly, automatically, lifted the covers and looked into the saucepans. After that she went to the table and put out the things they would need, the butter and salt; she looked in the refrigerator for the milk.

The milk was outside the house. She walked towards the back door slowly, her arm out in front of her; when she got to it she twisted the handle and pulled it open suddenly.

The man said: 'I'm thirsty. Can I have a drink of water?'

AT the entrance to the lock, Clara said: 'It's too late to go through. We've got to be back for lunch.'

'All right.' Sam was suddenly quiet, mollified. 'We'll come through this afternoon. We'll bring a picnic.'

'Will we? Will you come this afternoon, Susan?' Clara turned back, shouting. Susan raised her eyes to the sky, sighed at Wilkins. 'All right,' she said. 'It's pretty boring at home, actually.'

'We'll go back,' Sam said. 'Hold on. I just want to see Tom.'

He made Clara hold on to a hanging rope and ran up a flight of slimy stone steps to the side of the lock. A little group of people were standing there, watching the boats that came through the lock and the police launch by the island. The lock-keeper stood among them, his back resting on the long wooden handle of the lock gates. He looked down at the little boy who emerged from the steps going down to the water.

'Tom,' Sam said. 'How is it?'

The enormous man, whose belly hung in front of him surrounded with a belt like a horse's girth, had a pain in his stomach and felt tired as if he were going to die.

'Rough,' he said.

'Tom, they wouldn't let us land on the island. What's going on there, then?'

The lock-keeper leant back, his boots wedged against the iron steps, his buttocks pressed to the handle of the lock gates to open them. All the morning visitors, anglers, even reporters had been asking him about the island. No one asked him about his stomach. He was sick of them.

'Some tart over there,' he said, 'got done.'

'Can't quite say that, can we?' Campbell, still in his shorts, was returning to join the sightseers. He had been to the shop by the lock to buy some sweets and he walked with his thick fingers feeling into a small paper bag. 'After all, it may have been an accident. Hullo, youngster.'

Sam looked over to the island. There was a man in a soft hat walking up and down the roof of the boathouse, looking at the ground.

'If they want to find anything,' Sam said, 'they should look in our boathouse.'

Campbell secured a bull's-eye between two fingers, put it in his mouth and laughed. 'Who've you got in there, youngster? Jack the Ripper?'

Sam took no notice of him, following the lock-keeper as he pushed his way backwards to open the gate.

'We'll be through here this afternoon, Tom. Time for a talk?'

'I shouldn't think so. It's all go here today. All bloody go.'

When he turned the punt round Sam found the wind and the stream were against him. It was a good thing he hadn't gone any farther; in any case, it was going to take a long time to get home.

AFTERWARDS Julia wondered why she hadn't slammed the door and locked it; there was no foot inside, no intrusion. The man was a yard away from the back doorstep, standing in the middle of the path, his hands hanging at his sides, looking lost. She didn't say anything, and he repeated: 'I'm thirsty.'

She didn't shut the door because, above and behind her fear, she was curious, because she had to discover what was going to happen next. She went back into the kitchen and found him a glass, filled it at the tap. When she had filled it and turned round he was inside the house, he had come in silently, insidiously, but he was standing in the same position as if he had never moved. It was like the game she played with the children, when they had to move cautiously towards her, freezing like statues when she turned her head.

She handed him the glass and for a moment they both held it together; he became more real, like a shadow coming into focus, as he touched the glass she was holding. She felt able to look at him.

While he drank she saw that he was thin, that his hair was cut close to his skull and that his coat cuff was frayed. He had an identity disc round his thin, hairless wrist.

'Thank you.' He put down the glass and looked round. His eyes were small and quite colourless. The kitchen seemed to amuse him. 'Sometimes,' he said, 'they give me cigarettes.'

The groceries had just been delivered. She broke open the wrapping on a fresh box of a hundred cigarettes and offered him one.

He hesitated. 'I must warn you. I have absolutely no money.'

'That's all right.' She heard herself speaking from a long way off. 'Take one.'

'It's odd how if you tell people you have no money they start giving you things. You become like a dog or a cat, I suppose. No, I have got a match.' He lit his cigarette and began to smoke it hungrily, pulling it away from his mouth after each puff. 'I went round to the back door of the Station Hotel yesterday. Do you know, after a while they gave me a whole leg of chicken, and an extraordinary silver bowl full of peas? Quite surprising.'

He had a high, almost excited voice and a precise way of rounding off his words, as if each were a separate pebble that he was throwing away hard. Looking at him, Julia saw that his clothes were very old and he didn't seem to be wearing socks.

'I believe if you started asking them for money they'd give it to you. Just to show that they had it. Of course, you could only do that once. After that you'd have something yourself.'

He looked at her for some confirmation of this theory. She realized that he was quite young, younger than any man she now knew; young enough, possibly, to be her husband's son. Feeling something was expected of her, she said: 'Are you staying down here? Camping?'

He seemed grateful to her for asking him. 'I can sleep anywhere. As a matter of fact, I slept some of last night in your boathouse.'

She looked at him, finding nothing to say.

'Do you mind?'

'No. No, I suppose not.'

'People don't. Farther down the river I found a house with a studio in the garden. It was unlocked, so I spent the night in the studio on a couch. In the morning a man with a beard came in, he said: "What in hell's name are you doing here?" So I said I was sleeping on his couch. Then he went away and came back with breakfast on a tray.'

She still said nothing. In one way she felt older than him, in another she was like a child before a difficult and exacting uncle, she couldn't think of what to do, how to behave. He was sitting now on the edge of the table, and he had a way of saying everything as if it contained a profound truth. He added, leaning forward earnestly, 'Two eggs. With an egg cosy on the second one to keep it hot while I eat the first. This man kept hens. Amazing.'

When he talked he gripped the edges of the table. The best thing about him was the shape of his head and face, which was small and perfect, with almost feminine ears. The fear had gone now and Julia only felt an enormous uncertainty, a feeling of drifting away from everything that she knew and understood. All the loneliness, the routine of her existence seemed safe and desirable. If she was to talk to this man she must start again, start somewhere long before she married Swinton, almost when she was a child, pushed into a room of strange people, anxious to find out about them and yet knowing it was rude to point or ask questions. But before she could ask anything she was being questioned herself.

'Do you live here?'

'It's my house.'

'And all those cups with names on them?'

'They belong to the children.'

'How many children?'

'Three. And one friend of theirs is staying.'

'Extraordinary. Do you ever feel you want to leave, suddenly, disappear when they're all out of the house and never come back?'

'No.' As a matter of fact it was untrue; quite often she did, it was an idea she played with when their precarious, lethargic emotions, aroused and accumulating, seemed to suffocate her; when their demands dragged the youth and gaiety out of her like a long transfusion of blood. It was a feeling she had never admitted to herself, a thing she would never, by any chance, do.

'And is that what your husband drinks out of?'

'Yes.' It was an enormous, Victorian breakfast cup, covered with red and spiky roses, which they had found nestling on straw in a stall at a country fair. They had bought it before Susan was born, standing with their arms round each other's waists when they had only been married a year. It had never got broken and she took it down from the shelf to show him, thinking, perhaps, that he might be a wandering painter and would be interested. 'It's a nice thing. Do you like it?'

'I hate nice things.' He turned his head away suddenly, childishly, like a virgin who has been shown an obscene postcard. When he went on speaking he was speaking to the ground.

'And is it all very nice, the life that you and your husband live here? Is he faithful to you, do you think?'

At first she thought that she was going to break the cup, then she held it tightly to prevent it slipping out of her hands. She carried it back and put it on the shelf in front of the children's cups with their names painted on them.

'The children will be back soon,' she said. 'You'd better go.'

'I only said that because I don't know.' He stood up and came round the table behind her. 'It seemed to me interesting. I'm not married myself. I only wonder how people who are married get on with it.'

She turned off the stove, poured the potatoes into the colander in the sink. 'I must get on now,' she said. 'The children will be coming back.'

'That's what I mean.' The man was still behind her, talking. 'If you're a dog or a cat they give you chicken, boiled eggs, anything. Once you take an interest in them they don't like it. Under this couch I was telling you about there were a lot of empty whisky bottles, and when I asked the man with the beard if he used the place to come and drink in so that his wife wouldn't see, he turned me out. Naturally, I like to know things.'

Extraordinarily, she felt as if she had hurt his feelings and had better, in some way, reassure him.

'I don't mind what you say. I'm really busy, though.'

'I thought you minded. Hadn't you thought of it before?'

Of course, she told herself, she hadn't. Only that morning, when she saw Swinton off on the train, she realized how little she knew about him, about what he did with his day, who he had lunch with.

'If you must know, he is.' She turned the potatoes out into their dish. Then she began to chop parsley to go on them, vicious strokes, holding the knife at both ends.

'I'm glad.' He sat back on the edge of the table, relaxed. 'I tell you, I don't know about married people. I only had a sister, she wasn't married. A brother and sister, that's a strange relationship, don't you think?'

'I don't know.' She stopped chopping, scooped the parsley off the board.

'She was an actress. Not very good at it. I should think you would have been better.'

'Me? Why me?' She turned round, the knife in her hand.

'You've got all the movements. Slow, graceful, exaggerated. I would say you were very theatrical. I believe you practise grand death scenes when you think you're all alone.'

'You think that because you were watching.'

For the first time, he laughed. 'You've found me out,' he said. 'I like that. I like being found out.'

'Do you always spend your time spying on people?'

'Always.' He laughed again. 'But tell me. At one time you wanted to be an actress. You didn't really want to get married and live like this with' – he waved at the sideboard – 'with all these cups.'

She put the knife down on the draining-board, dried her hands on the apron hanging on the back of the kitchen door.

'Perhaps,' she said. 'A long time ago. But this is all much better. Now I can't talk any longer.'

'Why not? Don't you like it?'

She stood still, looking at him. He had been a diversion, a curious, unsettling interval in the dull pattern of her day. She still wanted to get back to her routine, to lay the table and go down to the river to watch for the children. And yet there was a curiosity, an interest in knowing what he was going to say next. He had pleased her, too, guessing about her wanting to be an actress, a thing that, for some reason, she had never told Swinton.

'I don't mind it,' she said. 'But you can't just talk all day.'

He laughed. 'You say foolish things, like my sister. I'll tell you what, though, we could talk more easily after you'd asked me to lunch.'

'I'm not going to ask you to lunch.'

'Why not?'

'Because of the children.'

'Wouldn't they like me?'

She considered him. 'Sam and Clara might. Susan has a friend from her school staying. She'd die of shame.'

'Is that,' he asked eagerly, 'because I'm not wearing any socks?'

She smiled suddenly, and for the first time she was at ease with him. She herself had found it difficult to live up to Susan and Wilkins.

'Couldn't I borrow a pair of your husband's?'

'No. That's impossible.'

'Then,' he said, hitting the side of the table hard and enthusiastically with the flat of his hand, 'I've thought of what I'll do.'

'What?' She was still smiling at him, a slow, tolerant and female smile. She thought that now he would go and she would be, in a small way, sorry.

He pointed out through the kitchen window to where the monkey-puzzle, a bizarre shape on the green lawn, cast a long shadow. 'I'll have lunch by myself out there, under that tree.'

'But why?'

'Don't you see. Then the children won't mind. There was a man near here, I cut his grass for him. I asked him for lunch but his wife wouldn't have me in the house, so they brought me my lunch out in the garden. Wonderful sort of tinned meat, cold.'

'But you haven't cut the grass.'

'I know. But I've talked to you. I've told you you could have been a great, great actress. Perhaps I've altered your life.' He was talking now very quickly and persuasively, the words still coming out with great clarity, like a hail of gravel on a closed window.

'But I can't give you lunch.' Her refusal somehow sounded weak, irrelevant. 'Haven't you got a home?'

'Of course I have. A room in London. It's got rather few walls, some people might call it a landing, but to me it's a room. You must come and see me there. Just now, I've had to be down here, I've had things to do, people to see. I'll tell you all about it when we've settled this lunch question. Besides' – he suddenly slowed down, looked out of the window again and then at her – 'I like it here. It's beautiful. It's the sort of place that inter-

ests me. You interest me so. I know you don't
like questions, but I would like to know some
more about you, about your children. Can they
act too?'

'Sam can,' she said; 'he does it all the time.'

'Interesting, that. And just let me ask you this
before I help you lay the table. Does it hurt very
much – having them, I mean?'

'Yes, of course.'

'Interesting. How interesting. That's just what
I'd always heard.'

'CYNTHIA.' Perkin Lorwood turned away from the window, a drying-up cloth in his ancient hand, to where his sister, still crowned with her inappropriate crocheted cap, was bending over the sink. 'I was perfectly right. Mrs Swinton has a visitor.'

'Nonsense, dear. She told us not.'

'He's out there. He's carrying a table out to the monkey-puzzle.'

'It must be Tom from the lock. He comes there to cut the grass sometimes.'

'No, dear. It's a far thinner man. He's putting the table down. Now he's going back into the house.'

'Really, you're just like that frightful man on the wireless describing the Boat Race.'

'Here he comes again.'

'Perkin, will you not look. The knives are just accumulating on the draining-board.'

'Upon my soul, I believe he's going to eat his lunch out there.'

'They often have their meals out.'

'But he's doing it all alone. And Cynthia – really, you must see this. It's too good.'

'Oh, what is it?' Her voice was testy, but she raised herself on her toes to look out of the small, steamy window of the bungalow's kitchen. Her brother brought his head close to hers to whisper in her ear: 'No socks.'

'Really?' Miss Lorwood stretched farther on to the tips of her toes, her tennis shoes squeaking under the strain. 'Do you suppose Mr Swinton knows?'

And then, as the man looked up from the table Perkin industriously returned to the draining-board.

'Come away now, Cynthia. We don't want him looking at us.'

'Well, really. And you've been gaping just as if he was the Coronation ever since lunch.'

'All right. I just don't care for him to look in on us.'

There was a silence as the washing-up water withdrew asthmatically from the sink to reappear, almost at once, and flood the gravel path outside the window.

'Do you know who he is, Perkin? Have you seen him before?'

Perkin was whistling over the knives. He paused thoughtfully. 'I don't think so. I really don't think I can have seen him. And I'm sure he can't have seen me.'

THE children disembarked like a defeated army brought off from a blood-stained and disastrous beachhead. Exhausted they staggered across the lawn and up to the house, dragging coats they hadn't needed behind them, leaving an odd sock and a shoe in the punt.

Sam led them, Clara followed, Susan and Wilkins brought up a disconsolate rear. They were hungry and taking a jaundiced view of the fact that Julia hadn't been by the boathouse to meet them.

When they got into the house they found the table unlaid and they slumped into their chairs, dropping their coats on the floor beside their places. Clara surveyed, with deep disapproval, the empty desert of mahogany.

'Hey,' she said, 'lunch doesn't seem to be ready.'

'Something,' said Sam, 'must have gone wrong.'

'I'm awfully sorry,' Susan said to Wilkins. 'Have you got your watch on?'

'Yes, I have. And it's twenty-five to two.'

'Really,' said Clara, 'as soon as Mummy's finished with the lunch she'll have to start getting our tea.'

Sam was sitting looking through the open door into the kitchen. He saw his mother come in through the back door with an empty tray. Then a curious thing happened. She stood looking out into the garden and suddenly and unexpectedly she curtsied.

Horrified, he heard her putting things on the tray in that part of the kitchen which was hidden from his view. She came into the dining-room smiling, the full tray in her hands.

'Good. You're back.'

They said nothing, sitting round the table like a committee of inquisitors about to try a particularly dangerous heretic. She looked at their faces in dismay, all her gaiety gone. They were none of them smiling.

At last Sam said: 'What were you dancing for?'

'Pick up the coats, Sam. And go and wash your hands.'

'I didn't put them there.'

'No, but pick them up. When you're back, we can begin.'

When he got back she was sitting at the head of the table, the children were still silent, but slightly less hostile at the sight of food.

When he had got his plate, Sam said: 'Well, what *were* you dancing for?'

She crumbled her bread and smiled ineffectively. 'I wasn't dancing, Sam. There's someone out in the garden. He's having his lunch out there. I took him something and he bowed to thank me. So I curtsied. It was very silly.'

The children stared, their forks in the air. Their eyes filled with despair. Julia gave a little cough.

'Now do get on with your lunch.'

Clara asked: 'There's who out in the garden?'

'Just a man, a man who came to the back door.'

'Why's he having lunch then?' Susan asked.

'He's – well, he's camping round here. I thought it would be kind to give him something. I think he's rather poor. Good heavens, you don't mind, do you?' She exploded finally, and they bent their heads, forking the food into their mouths with the unanimity of oarsmen.

'Did your friend enjoy the river?' Julia asked brightly, unable to bring herself to use the forbidding surname.

Wilkins paused to speak. 'It's nice for the kids here, isn't it? I expect they get some fun out of punting.'

'Yes, it's good for them. I expect you like the sea better?' Julia's eye strayed to the window.

'Actually, the sea bores me. I've got some cousins who live by the sea. I hate going to stay with them.'

Susan looked at her friend admiringly, the conversation lapsed.

Then Clara said: 'We want to go down past the lock this afternoon. Can we take a picnic?'

'Yes, of course you can. I'll get it ready after lunch.'

Sam said, as the result of long thought: 'I suppose he's still out there, eating?'

'Yes, he is. Sam, sit still.'

But the little boy had slithered from his seat and had run to the back door. He came back slowly, accusingly. When he had got back to his chair he said: 'It's my man. From the boathouse.'

The children looked from Sam to Julia, tense and eager, determined not to miss a word. Julia had a cigarette-box in front of her and she took a cigarette out, tapping it slowly on the lid as she spoke.

'Yes. He camps where he can. He was sleeping in the boathouse some of the night.'

Wilkins asked: 'Is he a tramp?'

'Well, in a sort of way. All sorts of people who haven't much money like to travel about and see different places. Writers and painters have done it. They depend on people like us to help them. They just feel it's a free, exciting life, that's all. Wouldn't you like to do it some day?'

'Sleep in the boathouse?' Clara shivered in an exaggerated manner. 'No, thanks awfully.'

CHILDREN, Julia thought, are so respectable.
They have all the failings of the middle classes,
they sit round in silence eating tasteless food, they
disapprove of anything new and strange. At the
moment, they were disapproving of her.

She gave Susan some more potatoes, white
mashed potatoes were what she liked, because
they had no taste and no flavour. They were the
sort of thing that Julia herself had liked, it was the
sort of lunch they had always had, a peaceful meal
without excitement, dedicated to the task of
clothing the children with flesh without shocking
their palates. That sort of life had kept her beautiful, preventing her breasts from sagging or the
corners of her mouth from drooping, and the
only lines round her eyes had been where she
screwed up her eyes to smile. It suited her, she
knew, the love of her husband which had become
detached, amused almost, with time, but
remained solid and dependable and secure so that,
she felt certain, he would never be cruel to her or

betray her or let her suffer. And the children suited her, filling the house so that she wept to herself if one of them went away to stay, or when they went back to school. Together they made her what she was, a woman of thirty-eight, beautiful because she had never, seriously, been unhappy.

And yet today there was the feeling of dissatisfaction, of emptiness, or longing. When she had heard the man talk, when she had taken him his lunch and seen him bow, she had seemed to see opening before her a life of absurdity and freedom and pain, the life that a well-brought-up child might see from behind the locked gates of a convent school, knowing that she will grow up and never have shared in it at all.

The children ate their pudding, the girls, even Wilkins, arranging their cherry stones methodically to forecast their marriage to tinkers, sailors or thieves, characters they would, in all probability, never encounter. Julia removed a grain of tobacco from her lip with one fingernail, thinking that his questions, ridiculous as they were, had freed her a little from the things that she loved and believed in, like her questions about God which had freed her, little by little, from the necessity for belief. She wondered why, in a curious way, his arrival had added excitement to her day.

She knew, when she thought about it, that she didn't want him to go away. That he had stilled, for an hour, the fear and regret that was somewhere in her, the regret that she had existed and grown and grown beautiful only for this, for a husband who had become used to the idea and for children who didn't notice it; the fear that her beauty had only a few years to last and that she, Julia Swinton, must presently die.

She looked automatically at the children's plates. 'Sam,' she said, 'you haven't eaten your cherries.'

'They're sour. Very horrible and sour.'

Clara said: 'What about the picnic?'

'Help clear away. Then I'll get it.'

SAM stacked the dirty plates and carried them into the kitchen. He felt angry and lost and robbed. For a little while he had had something, a secret, a stranger, possibly a friend. Now it was all gone, it had become his mother's. She had taken the man away from them, she was hiding him from them.

When they got into the kitchen they found that he had brought in his plates and washed them up. Wilkins and Susan stood grimly beside the sink with drying-up cloths, Julia tied the apron round her waist. Sam sidled out of the back door, found a stone in the path and kicked it. In a little while Clara joined him; he looked at her with hate.

'Go back,' he said, 'and do the washing-up.'

'No. Why should I?'

'It's a girl's job.'

'No, it would be unfair if I did it. I did it last Thursday.'

'Go away, then. I'm busy.' He put his hands in

his pockets, walked after the stone and kicked it again.

All the same, she followed. 'Where are you going?'

'I'm going to see the man.'

'Why can't I come?'

'Because he wouldn't like you. He hates girls.'

'How do you know?'

'Tom told me. Tom at the lock.'

'Liar.'

'Go away or I'll kill you.'

'You couldn't. You couldn't even try.'

Then, as they came round the corner of the house, they were silent. The man was lying under the tree, apparently asleep. They stood on the path and watched him, separated from him by a long stretch of lawn as green and quiet as a quiet sea.

Clara stayed on the path. Both children waited a long time, watching, then Sam slowly left her. He walked across the grass with care, holding his arms a little away from his sides as if he were walking on a tightrope and had to balance. Ten yards from the tree he stopped. The man was flat on the ground, his coat rolled and pushed under his head for a pillow, his chest rising and falling under the checked shirt, his hips thin and his thighs narrow, his legs stretched out in cheap brown striped trousers, his bare ankles growing painfully out of heavy, dusty shoes. Sam tiptoed forward. He came nearer, fascinated by the sight of eyelids closed over hard eyeballs, by the set, unsmiling face and close-cropped hair. The man was pale in the shadows, and the reflection of light from the leaves and the grass gave his flesh a greenish colour, as if he had been drowned. Sam was quite near now, looking down on the face which appeared to him upside down, the chin and mouth above the forehead. Yes, he said to himself; yes, it's him all right.

Then, as he looked, the man opened one eye. The pupil shot back, looking at the boy standing behind him, leaving the white eye below it. And then the eye closed.

Sam jumped backwards. When he had recovered he took another step nearer.

'Are you asleep?' he asked.

But the man didn't answer, sunk back, apparently, into the deepest trance.

Sam ran back to the kitchen. The washing-up was finished, his mother was cutting sandwiches, the coffee machine was bubbling on the stove.

'Hurry up, Sam. The others have all gone to get ready. Where have you been?'

'Seeing the man again.' He came near to the table, found half a tomato and ate it.

'Have you?' She was stirring the coffee in the top of the glass machine and she didn't turn round. Then she turned off the gas and let the coffee run down into the bowl. 'What was he doing?'

'Pretending to be asleep.'

'Really? How do you know he was pretending?'

'I caught him out, opening one eye.'

'Why would he pretend to be asleep?'

She turned away from the stove and got two cups off the shelf.

'I don't know why. He's peculiar, isn't he?'

'Oh, not really. I don't think so. Here, take him out a cup of coffee. He might like it.'

Sam took the coffee and held the cup and saucer with both hands so as not to spill it. When he got out to the tree again and the man had gone. He put the cup of steaming coffee on the grass under the monkey-puzzle and left it there, tiptoeing away like a small and primitive native who has, in the place of a sacred and unseen presence, left an offering for the god.

SUSAN lay on her bed while Wilkins unlatched her suitcase to find another cardigan. She would have liked to stay there all the afternoon, in the hot, stuffy bedroom which smelt of caramels and face powder. She and Wilkins could have got out the long, school photograph in which, by a triumph of arrangement on trestles and chairs, by a subtle gradation of squatting, kneeling, standing on the ground and standing on objects, three hundred and fifty girls had been caught in one photograph. They could have discussed the three hundred and fifty one by one, finding in the identical circular faces over the tussore shirts and straight knitted ties, objects of envy, hatred and love. Susan looked out at the bright afternoon; if only it would rain there might be a chance of doing it.

'I'm sorry about Mummy,' she said. 'She doesn't often do things like this. Hardly ever, in fact.'

'When we have tramps,' Wilkins examined

herself in the mirror; inexorably, in a day's time, she was going to have a spot on the side of her nose, 'Mummy sends them away.'

'We do usually, too.' Susan's voice became anxious, almost desperate. 'I can't understand it at all. I know Daddy wouldn't like it.'

Susan said this hopefully, in fact she had little faith that Swinton, who was capable of dressing at breakfast, would not have been worse than her mother with the tramp. On Saturdays he often took Tom down to the pub after Tom had finished in the garden, a habit which was distasteful to Susan whose ideas of social equality were rooted in the novels of Jane Austen.

'If anyone in the neighbourhood got to know about lunch today,' Susan went on, 'it would be quite disastrous.'

'Don't worry.' Wilkins sounded aloof. 'He's probably your long-lost cousin or something.'

'Of course he's not. We know all our cousins.'

'Well, this might be one you'd forgotten. Turned up from Australia or somewhere. Perhaps,' Wilkins went on casually as if, in this house, nothing could surprise her, 'he's escaped.'

'Escaped from where?'

There was a moment of hostility before Wilkins decided not to press her advantage and Susan stopped herself from saying that even if, by some horrible mischance, she had a cousin from Australia at least she hadn't, as it was rumoured Wilkins had, an uncle who was a vet.

'Oh, I don't know,' Wilkins went on vaguely.

'Perhaps he's just a tramp after all. I know some parents can't cope with that sort of thing.'

'He'll be gone by teatime,' Susan promised hopefully. 'It's really too bad on your first day. Look, shall we take the photograph down to the boat. We can take some scissors and cut out our specials.'

'If you like.'

'And, Wilkins . . .'

'Yes?'

'You will walk with me next term, won't you?'

'Oh, *je ne sais*.' Wilkins was vague. 'Do you suppose he'll stay to tea?'

'Who?'

'The tramp.'

'Of course not. Come on, let's go down.'

'All right. I suppose we'd better go and keep the kids happy. Come on then.'

Susan followed Wilkins, doubtful if, when Wilkins had finished her visit, she would still be in the ten specials cut out of Wilkins's photograph. She felt sad and yet resentful of Wilkins; after all, she could see, in spite of what she had said, that her mother meant to be kind. As the two girls wandered down the staircase and out into the sun they drew away from each other and Susan felt her friendship cooling, a sure step in the process of growing up, a step towards the day when she would fall in love and have no friends left at all.

'WHERE do I put the basket? In the end?'

'In the bows, Mummy, you mean.'

Julia knelt on the edge of the lawn and lowered the white basket into the punt. The swans, seeing food, sailed up to the boat, fluttering their back feathers and looking down their black beaks with the viciousness of sirens in early silent films. Behind them the cygnets floated, ugly and self–conscious and young. Julia pushed the boat away with her hand and Sam paddled it out into the centre of the river, the swans hissing disappointment behind him. Julia rose from her knees and walked back across the lawn; as he turned his head Sam saw the man come out of the boathouse and walk towards her. They met in the middle of the lawn, alone in the garden.

He asked: 'You've sent them all away?'

'I didn't send them. They went.'

'Were they upset by me?'

'They're very conventional. They don't like anything out of the ordinary.'

'So they were upset. The little boy came up to me and wanted to talk, but I pretended to be asleep.'

'Why?'

'I couldn't think of anything to say to him.'

It was true, she thought, you have to reach a certain age before you talk to children when you first see them. Children, when they first meet, back away from each other silently, like dogs, and this man had about him an instinctive callousness which was like a child's. When he spoke again she was surprised, almost shocked.

'Are you busy? Shall I go away now?'

She didn't want to ask him to stay; it hurt her and made her feel ridiculous.

'I'm not very busy, Come in, if you like.'

'What will you give me?'

She started to get angry, and then decided to treat it as funny. 'I don't know. A drink?'

'That would be exciting. Why do you get angry at having to ask me in? Why does it make you angry having to say what you want to say?'

She didn't answer and he followed her into the house, into the sitting-room.

'You always have to pretend to be different from what you are. You're like my mother, my father too.'

'What were they like?' She opened the cupboard and looked at the bottles, three beer bottles with screw tops, a cider bottle half-empty that they had brought home from a picnic, some gin and Italian vermouth, something left in a Dubon-

net bottle and a bottle of cognac. 'What would
you like to drink?'

'Whatever's the most expensive.'

She gave him some cognac, a wine glass half-
full. She gave herself some too; she had had
women friends who drank brandy in the after-
noons, but up to then she hadn't dared to do so
herself. She put off the thought of what she would
tell Swinton, or whether she should even try filling the bottle up with water. The day still seemed
to her isolated, like a holiday, its consequences
unimportant.

'You were going to tell me,' she said, 'about
your mother and father.' Talking to him was difficult; she used catch phrases, sentences that she
would have introduced into any conversation
with her or her husband's friends. He never gave
the right answer.

'They're awful. I haven't seen them for a long
time. My sister, I believe, used to sometimes get
letter-cards. Do you know those terrible things
that stick up all along the sides?'

'I'm sure they aren't. What's so awful about
your mother and father?'

'You know. Middle-class agnostics. Very tolerant about everything.' He was standing up and
he gulped the brandy suddenly. She looked up at
him from her seat on the arm of a chair; his eyes
were bright and his cheeks were flushed slightly,
like a girl's. 'Before I left home for the last time I
said to my father, "I hate you. And what's more,
I'm going to go and confess my hatred of you to a

priest.'' That was the only part he minded. Priests shocked him.'

She frowned at him, sipping the brandy which went down her throat like a warm, clean gust of wind. 'Do you believe in God, then?'

'Of course not. But I wasn't going to tell my father that. I kept that to tell the priest.'

'And did you tell the priest?'

'Yes. One at the far end of Buckingham Palace Road. I went into his little box and whispered in his ear: "God doesn't exist." He didn't seem to hear, just said: "Say five Hail Marys." You know the sort of thing.'

He put his hands together in a ridiculous imitation of prayer. She laughed, doubting if the story were true. He became serious again, looking at her with his eyes almost closed. 'You know,' he said, 'you're very beautiful. Far more than my sister. Or perhaps in a different way. It made you feel sad to look at her, like thinking of things you've missed. You, on the other hand, give me a contented feeling.'

The smiles made wrinkles again at the corners of her eyes.

'But you'd have thought her beautiful, I'm sure. She looked as if she'd break if you touched her and yet she must have been strong. And she had a way of looking very young and quite old at the same time. No one could stop looking at her.'

Vaguely Julia remembered that it was the second time that day that someone had seemed to be appealing to her to admit the beauty of a girl

she had never seen. She had a feeling that the conversation had happened before, that she knew, if
she put her mind to it, what was going to happen
next.

'What's your sister got to do with it?'

'That was typical. My father was a doctor, you
know, solid general practitioner.' He sat on the
sofa, putting his glass on the floor. 'Got his beliefs
from having dissected a stomach without being
able to find a soul. Now I told you my sister was
an actress, she met a lot of people and went out.
At one time she had a love-affair with someone
and later she had to have, what's the word they
use? – an abortion?'

'You don't mean to say your father – ?' She was
puzzled by the story, as much as by his strange
ignorance.

'Oh, he didn't do it. But he knew about it, he
knew all about it and he took a very enlightened,
tolerant attitude. Of course he did, he didn't want
another child to keep. So after she'd had it, the
operation, they brought her home and kept her
in bed, they even built her up with beef tea. That
was when I left.'

'What do you think they should have done?'
Julia asked, still not understanding. 'Turned her
out of the house?'

'Of course. If they hadn't killed her.'

'You're joking.'

'Am I?' He went to the cupboard, filled his
glass. 'Perhaps I am. I don't want to say things
you don't like. I didn't mean it when I said you

were like them. You are kind and not just tolerant. Look at you giving me this brandy.'

'Yes, look at me. What will my husband say?'

'What will he? What will he say when the children tell him I had lunch under the tree?'

'Nothing very much, I don't suppose.'

'Is he tolerant too?'

'Very tolerant.'

'How dull.'

'Why?' she laughed. 'Do you think I should be
killed too, in a jealous rage?'

'Perhaps.' He sat down on the sofa opposite
her, his legs stretched out in front of him, holding
his glass in both hands. 'But, no, of course not.
You're too good for that. Nothing like that
should happen to you.'

Outside the sun shone so brightly that a sun-
beam, strengthened by a pane of the window as
if by a magnifying glass, falling on her hand was
unbearably hot. She moved from the arm of the
chair into its depths, and sank back into the
shadows. It was a moment, in the house surrounded by silence, when the day seemed to have
stopped, the clock on the mantelpiece was
motionless and the shadow of the tree on the lawn
fixed. It was like the moment of stillness when a
toboggan reaches the crest of a slope and seems
to pause before the final descent. In it, she felt,
everything or nothing could happen.

He got up from his seat and came over to her
chair, squatting in front of her on his heels. She
had an instinct to put out her hand and feel his

hair; it looked short and brittle and she wanted to know how it felt. But she said nothing and did nothing, waiting for him to move.

The time was motionless, the suspense of everything about her complete; but she felt calm, as if the decision were not hers. She couldn't tell if suddenly, in the silence that enveloped them, her day was going to change and she was going to move, without warning, into a world which she and her husband had grown past and never experienced. However, she was ready and unapprehensive because, since the beginning of the day, she seemed to have come so far.

Then he spoke again and almost at once the clock moved on; the shadow on the lawn lengthened. For the first time he had made an odd retreat from her, his eyes moved away and sideways. He stood up.

'I'd like to see you do it again.'

'Do what again?'

'The business with the dagger.'

She was relieved, saddened, puzzled by what she felt. As he moved away from her and across the room he lost reality, for the first time since she had met him after lunch she thought of the children on the river, of what she was going to cook for Swinton's dinner.

'I can't now, in cold blood.'

He looked round at her. 'Is there any play where that really happens? Where a woman stabs herself?'

She thought, frowning: 'I can't think of one. Cleopatra did it with a snake.'

He turned round fully, excited and interested. 'Did she? Did she really? Do you know the words?'

But her thoughts were wandering as she looked out towards the river.

'I learnt them once,' she said. 'I've forgotten them all now.'

TOM at the lock went into the front room of his house, which was fitted up as a shop. On the table by the window were bars of chocolate, tins of potato crisps, bottles of soft drinks and terrible-looking buns in glass cases. On the wallpaper, decorated with a repeating pattern of parrots, hung two advertisements for Coca Cola, a photograph of King George V and a photograph of himself when young. In this photograph he was sitting in a skiff, peering angrily out from behind a curled moustache. He was wearing a singlet and long stockings with knickerbockers. In that year he had won the watermen's sculls and beaten the record for the river.

He didn't feel like that now. He felt old and awful in the stomach. He went over to a cupboard in which he kept his medicines, castor oil, milk of magnesia, port and brandy. He belched and then mixed up some port and brandy and drank it. It didn't make him feel much better.

He lived alone now, sleeping alone in the big

bed with brass handles like a coffin where his wife had died. He cooked his own food and mended his own clothes and felt too tired to do the garden, so that for the first year the name of the lock wasn't picked out in snapdragons in the bed by the river. He had no friends left among the boatmen and he was scared of dying in the middle of the night.

He found the end of a Woodbine, lit it and coughed. Then he opened a bottle of lemonade, poured it into a cloudy glass and took it out to the man who was sitting at one of the iron tables by the lock.

'This the best you can do for me?'

'We got no licence.'

'All right. Have a seat.'

Tom sat down reluctantly. He knew who this man was, a thin man with a yellowish face, puzzled brown eyes and a straggling moustache that seemed to have alighted on his upper lip like a rare insect, causing him equal resentment and surprise. The man spoke in an educated voice and had leather cuffs and elbow-pads on his tweed coat.

Tom asked: 'You finished over there, then?'

At times he hated the punts, the men who never ought to have taken off their shirts and the silly bitches lying about in sunglasses. More than them he hated the police.

'Not quite.'

Tom belched again and the man looked up from his fizzy lemonade. 'Tummy trouble?'

'Rough today. Can't seem to quieten it.'

'Have a peppermint. We all depend so much on them in this bloody country now, don't we?'

The policeman handed peppermints, without looking at Tom, as if he were passing the necessary but secret stem of the opium pipe. He gazed out at the river, the deep-blue sky, the dark, wet green of the trees, in despair. England for him was the mortgage on his house, the slowness of promotion, the nagging of his wife and the grocer's bill. During the war he had been in Africa, about the only place left which bore, as far as he could make out, any relation to life at Brighton College.

'Peaceful sort of job you've got here.'

'Peaceful! Don't you believe it. All bloody go.'

Get a couple of natives on this lock now, and they'd open and shut the damn thing eighteen hours a day and thank you for it. Give the job to an Englishman and he couldn't even keep the garden tidy.

'Perhaps you can help me.'

His father, who had taught him the unexpectedness of life by putting a penny under his pillow and then stealing it back from him while he was asleep, had taught Tom never to say anything to the police. He looked up sideways, his eyes bright and slanting in an ancient, wrinkled face. 'What do you mean?'

'Perhaps you saw someone come off that island last night? Young chap, not too well dressed. Mean anything to you?'

'Can't say it does.'

Tom looked down at his foot. They always lied, the policeman thought, and over here there was nothing you could do about it.

'How did that girl get over to her houseboat?'

'There's a dinghy,' Tom answered cautiously; the question seeemed harmless enough.

'Only one.'

'As far as I know.'

'That'll be the one the charwoman used this morning.'

'Suppose so. Sam!' Tom suddenly shouted to the little boy as he came up the steps again to the lock. 'How is it, boy?'

'All right. We've had tramps for lunch. Now we're going through for a picnic. Can I have some crisps?'

'I'll get them for you.' Tom pushed himself up from his chair. When they were alone the man turned to the boy, questioning him as he stood to attention before the table as if he were a tribesman of doubtful loyalty from the reserve.

'Hallo, son. What did you say you had for lunch?'

'Only a tramp came. One, in fact.'

Down in the lock, the policeman saw, there was a punt full of girls. He wondered, not knowing the dialect, whether it was worth while continuing the interrogation.

'Live round here, do you?'

'River House, Marsh Road, Lemming.'

'Have you seen this tramp before?'

Tom came out of the house; by looking at him Sam could tell that this was a man they didn't like. He lied wildly. 'Oh, lots of times. He often comes.'

'Really?'

'Stays the night sometimes, we all like him so.'

Now he knew he'd gone too far, he looked hard at Tom, longing to say the right thing. He put a crisp in his mouth; by some influence of the river it was wet and flabby. He was proud to be with Tom and he wanted to show the strange, inquisitive man that he and Tom were old friends. He took no notice of Clara, calling him from the punt.

'Mother at home, is she?'

'I expect she's gone out.'

'Be back this afternoon?'

'She may be.'

The policeman leant forward and continued the questioning, pressed on by his indigestion, the repayments to the building society, the tea parties his wife liked to give to her friends: the old man grinned behind his hand, the boy invented wildly, the girls called from the punt.

Tom said: 'She's busy, though, isn't she, Sam? Come on. Let's get those girls out of the way.'

'I've got to paddle them all the way.'

'Tiring, eh? Paddling three girls at once?' Tom leaned back in his chair and hit the iron table with an enormous flat hand. On his way into the house he had tried the brandy alone and he felt better.

'Did you see this tramp last night at all?'

'Three at once, eh? Very tiring, I'd call that. Most tiring, isn't it, Sam boy?' Sam looked betwildered, the policeman stared out across the water. Tom laughed until his eyes disappeared into his cheeks and he went scarlet and then purple as he started to cough. He ended his laugh by gasping for breath, feeling cold and desperate.

'He comes when he likes. We all like him.'

'Old man?'

'Not so old.'

'Let's get your boat through. Can't have the river littered up like this.'

Sam saw Tom get to his feet, pressing himself up from the table. He followed him to the edge of the lock, feeling that he had made a mistake and wondering what it was. By the water Tom stopped and looked down at the punt.

'All sitting there,' he said, 'like a bloody sewing bee. Afternoon, ladies.'

Wilkins looked up coldly, Clara waved, Sam ran on to the gates and started turning the wheels. Tom came after him to help.

'Did I say something wrong?' Sam whispered, looking past him at the man at the table who, finishing his lemonade, picked up his hat and left.

'He wants to know too bloody much.' Tom finished turning the wheel, adding, as if it explained everything: 'Anyway, I feel rough.'

'You ought to go and lie down.'

'Do that in my box, can't I?' He laughed again, but not as if it were funny.

When it came to closing the gates Sam pushed

as hard as he could to help the man whose strength seemed to be draining out of him. He stuck his arms straight out in front and pushed, his head down, his eyes glued to Tom's great boots, iron capped and slithering on the gravel like the hooves of a cart horse that can no longer grip the road. When they had got the gates shut, Tom stood with his back to the long wooden boom, his shirt was dark with sweat and his face looked grey. Sam liked him better than anyone he knew, better than his father and mother, much better than his sisters, but seeing him like that he backed away, instinctively frightened like a dog smelling death.

'Can't do you any good, boy, talking to his sort.'

They turned the wheels at the far end of the lock and the water poured in, bringing the punt slowly and gracefully up to the level of the over-grown garden. Then they opened the gates and Sam got into the punt. When he pushed off Tom was leaning over the boom, his dead cigarette stuck against his top lip, his cap pushed on to the back of his head.

'Keep going, boy,' he shouted. 'Don't do any-thing I wouldn't do.'

'Why were you so long?' Clara asked. 'What did Tom say?'

'He's rough. Let's get on, quickly.'

As he left the gate Tom saw that a launch had drawn up and was moored at the entrance to the lock. On the miniature deck Campbell lay without a shirt on, his eyes closed under his glasses and a rubber pillow under his head.

'Coming through?' Tom shouted down to him.

'Not just now.' Campbell seemed suddenly to have woken up. 'I'm staying here for just now.'

'YOU look disappointed. Do you feel unhappy now?'

'Of course not.'

'You're disappointed perhaps, because you can't do Cleopatra's speech.'

'Nothing like that at all.' She laughed at him and moved over to the window, looking out at the sunshine. 'It's hot. What an extraordinary day it's been.'

'Because I came, of course, not because of the sun.'

She looked round at him, at his thin body in the cheap clothes, skull-like head and wide-open eyes.

'You're conceited,' she said. 'What about?'

'Only because I'm alone. Not tied up' – his eyes moved round the room – 'with all this sort of thing.'

'You may be one day.'

'Never. Never at all.'

'You think,' Julia said, 'I should have been different. More like – well, more like your sister?'

'Be what you want. What you feel you have to be. That's the only thing.'

She shook her head slowly, standing by the window. 'Of course it's not . . .' And she was going to say more but the telephone interrupted her.

She went out of the sitting-room into the front hall and closed the door behind her. She looked at the little furious instrument, wondering why it sounded so angry, and then lifted it slowly. When she heard the voice she blinked, taken by surprise.

'Hallo, darling. You asked me to telephone you.'

Swinton sounded far away, but curiously gentle and conciliatory.

'Oh, yes. About this evening. Shall I come to the station?'

'Well.' There was a pause. She heard the man moving behind the shut door of the sitting-room. 'No, better not. I'll walk or get a taxi. I still don't quite know what time it'll be.'

She was listening to his footsteps going away. She didn't answer.

'I'm afraid it's rather vague.'

'Oh, no. It's all right.'

'Goodbye, then. Everything all right?'

'Yes. Fine.'

'See you this evening.'

She waited. Then she drew in a breath. 'Look,

I suppose I ought to tell you . . .' she began, but
he had cut off, there was silence.

She put back the receiver reverently, cautiously, as one might replace in its cage a small
animal which has unexpectedly died. Then she
opened the door and walked back into the sitting-
room. It was empty, the other door and the doors
of the back hall, the kitchen and dining-room and
the door into the back garden, were all open.
Nothing moved in the house and not even the
smallest wind from the garden stirred the papers
on Swinton's desk.

He had gone suddenly, and there was nothing
to explain her sadness, the feeling of emptiness
that surrounded her. She took the brandy glasses
out to the kitchen and washed them. He had gone
and nothing had happened, her day was left to
her, her life had been unmolested, unchanged. He
was walking, she thought, out along the dusty
road, peering inquisitively at back doors and in at
windows, he would continue his journey and she
would never, in her whole life, do anything different.

Thinking of it, she forgot a small disappointment, a slight dissatisfaction that she had felt with
him at the end. Once again he was strange and
disconcerting and she wanted, once more, to
listen to him and think about the unexpected
things he said, she wanted to put out her hand and
touch him, and she regretted that she hadn't done
this when she had the opportunity.

In the kitchen she looked up at the row of cups

with the children's names painted on them. He had laughed at that and indeed, she thought, how middle class that is, how smug, always to put your name on your possessions. She thought that when the time came for her to tell Swinton about the man having lunch she would make light of it, present it to him as a joke, trivial and unimportant, and the thought of how she would do this made her feel isolated and alone. Swinton would smile, as he did at her mild extravagances or eccentricities, and the day would be over, forgotten.

And yet as the memory of the man receded, as she thought how it was all over, passed without any incident, her feeling of regret mingled with relief, relief because she was back, firmly and for ever, in the life that was most familiar to her. She was like someone who is sure of feeling faintly unwell, so that they can, with a good conscience, put off going to a party which they are both looking forward to and dreading.

All the same she found the idea of the man hard to relinquish and she thought about him, holding the glasses under the hot tap, standing them upside down on a tray and then wiping them as carefully as a criminal might wipe, in order to remove all fingerprints, the instruments of his crime. She became sure that he hadn't gone very far. Again she had the feeling that he was near to her, still in the garden, possibly watching her, and at the thought she felt, now, not frightened but reassured. It was as if, while he was still there, the matter was not finally concluded or the day returned to normal.

When the front-door bell rang it didn't surprise her and she wiped her hands slowly before she went to answer it. But when she opened the door it was another stranger, thin and anxious, gazing from behind his moustache with eyes that looked mystified and betrayed.

'Mrs Swinton?'

'Yes.'

'I'm from the police, madam. Could I take a minute of your time?'

'Yes, of course. Would you like to come in?'

It was extraordinary to see him sitting on the sofa where the man had been. His nostrils twitched as he looked round the room. It seemed to reassure him. The bottle was still open on the table.

'Would you like a drink?'

'No, thank you. I daren't start it. Like smoking, once I started that I'd be a victim to it. Of course, the wife has to smoke. This is a dreadful country, isn't it, for a woman?'

She couldn't imagine what he was talking about, what he had come for, and yet she was patient, waiting to find out.

'I'm over here on this sad business of Miss Paneth. I expect you knew her.'

'Miss Paneth?'

'She had a houseboat near here. Unfortunately she had some sort of . . . She was found dead.'

To understand she would have to forget the

important part of the day, remember what seemed to her trivialities. She screwed up her eyes, seeing the big face of Campbell again, hearing the words that had frightened her; why they had frightened her she found now difficult to remember.

'I heard something about it this morning, from a friend of ours at the station.'

'Really?' His eyes cast about the room, anxious and inquisitive. 'Only one point I wanted to bother you about. Someone saw a stranger, a young chap, thin, shabbily dressed, on the towpath last night. Anyone like that called on you?' He asked the question without looking at her, as if, in his investigations, he was more furtive than the quarry he pursued.

It was ridiculous, but she meant to lie, why she had no idea, but instinctively she meant to say 'no'; it was as if some obscure point of honour were involved. Before she could speak his eyes met hers for a moment and he said: 'I may say I've seen the good lady and gentleman next door. They spoke of someone sitting under your tree.'

It was no longer ridiculous but sad, sad that she should have to tell the story like this, so soon after it was all over. It was like the wonderful days she had had out as a child and, as soon as she had got home, her mother had said: 'Come on, now, tell us all about it. Tell us exactly what you did.'

'Well, yes. He called here this morning.'

'What time would that be?'

'Oh, just before lunch. About half-past twelve.'

'Twelve-thirty. He hadn't been here before that?'

'That was the first time I saw him.'

'When did he leave?'

'Just now. Five minutes ago.'

The man's eyes flickered to the French clock on the mantelpiece.

'Two forty-five. Is it true you gave him some refreshment?'

'I gave him some lunch. Afterwards, he came in here and had a drink.'

'Had you met him before today?'

'No. Never.'

'The good lady said he was dressed very poorly, like a tramp.'

'Yes.'

The man searched in his moustache with a fingernail. Julia began to feel angry and unhappy, as if he had told her she had made a fool of herself.

'That's to say,' she qualified herself, 'he was untidy. I know a don who dresses worse.'

'I dare say. Poor, too?'

'I shouldn't think he had much money.'

The man pulled in his bottom lip and bit it with his teeth.

'You were very charitable, Mrs Swinton. Very kind and charitable, I'm sure.'

'Not a bit. He – he was very interesting.'

'Talked a good deal?'

'Yes.'

'What about?'

'Really . . .' She gestured helplessly, an unlit

cigarette in one hand, a matchbox in the other.
'Really, I can't remember it now.'

'Mention his sister at all?'

He was watching her, and she lit the cigarette
thoughtfully. She lied, not in order to mislead
him, but because she wanted to keep something
of their meeting private, to herself.

'No. I don't think so.'

'See him there?'

She looked at the photograph he gave her, two
people in basket chairs on a lawn, the man wearing a white jacket and glasses, a panama hat in his
lap, the woman elderly and anxious wearing a
cardigan and a tweed skirt. Behind them stood
her visitor of the morning, younger, not so thin.
There was a Sealyham lying on the grass. In the
foreground, dark and shapeless, was the shadow
of the girl who had taken the photograph.

'Where did you get this?'

'She had it stuck in the frame of a mirror in her
bedroom. See the likeness? Father, mother and
brother, I suppose, they'd be. Do you recognize
him?'

This time she hated the thought of him prowl-
ing into other people's bedrooms, unfixing their
photographs. She hated the thought, and she
wasn't going to help.

'No, I don't think so.'

He said nothing. The silence was so long that
she felt that she had to speak to break it.

'Was there something – extraordinary about
the way she died?'

'Did you hear that?'

'No.'

'Who did you say told you about it?'

'A friend of ours. Mr Campbell. He has a launch down here.'

There was another silence. The man got up.

'I've heard about him. That's Campbell of the animal quizzes on the wireless, isn't it?'

'Yes.'

'We always listen to that.' He frowned. 'Wonderfully agile brain. Those puns. Wonderfully agile.'

'I believe so. I've never heard him.'

'Apart from those programmes, the wife says, and Selfridges, you can keep England.'

He looked round at the furniture; nice pieces, he thought, and all paid for, no doubt. This woman should have been on the right side, but here you could never tell. Not like a decent country, where the criminals were inside the prohibited areas and the girls took their revolvers to the tennis club. He hadn't even been able to decide, on that crazy houseboat, whether it was a crime at all.

'No,' he said. 'She died all right. There's a rotten old staircase up to the roof of her houseboat and she fell down it, broke her neck at the bottom. From the empty bottles we found round the place I wonder if she was all that sober at the time.'

She stood up, relieved, to show him out. 'Then it all seems quite simple.'

He had wandered away from her to the far end

of the room. She saw his fingers, thin and yellow-ish, brush the surface of a table. The hand looked to her, for a moment, like an insect, dangerous and intrusive, alighting on the objects in the dead girl's bedroom, on her own furniture during an afternoon which she had wanted to think over quietly ever afterwards, in secret. His voice was a remote, threatening buzz of words, only partly intelligible to her.

'There was only one thing we couldn't quite work out. Of course, we may have been stupid about it and there may be a simple explanation. But do you happen to know how she got to and from this island?'

'Not at all.'

'There was one little boat, a rowing dinghy. Now the charwoman who found Miss Paneth dead – she comes up the towpath every morning at eight, then she rings a bell on the landing stage opposite the houseboat and Miss Paneth, or who-ever's there, comes over in the dinghy to fetch her.'

'I didn't know. We really don't know her at all.' She was only half-listening to him, looking out to the monkey-puzzle tree and wondering if the white thing she could see underneath it could possibly be a cup.

'Well, this morning the woman didn't have to ring. The boat was there and she rowed herself across. When she got to the houseboat she found Miss Paneth and she telephoned to us.'

It was a cup and Julia thought one of the most curious things about the day.

'So the only thing that worries me is, how did the boat get there? Miss Paneth would hardly have rowed it over when she was dead.'

'So what do you want to find out?'

'Who was with her. That's all. Who was with her when she died.'

He had left the photograph on the table by the brandy bottle. Julia looked again at the shadow on the grass. She tried to imagine the girl who had come home for the weekend bored and a little irritated by her parents, missing the lover who came to her flat in London, suddenly, in a moment when she was trying to get on with them, photographing them, catching them looking at her anxiously, hoping for the best, and behind them the face of her brother who had said, when he talked about her, that she ought to be killed.

'I'm sorry I couldn't help you any more.'

'That's all right, Mrs Swinton. You did your best, I'm sure. Only if you should see him again –'

'Yes?'

'Just ring us at once, will you? I'll leave the number by the telephone.'

His hand picked up the photograph. He turned to look at her.

'I'd advise you to do that, Mrs Swinton, in the interests of your own safety I'd advise you to do it.'

It was only after he had gone that Julia understood exactly what he had told her.

'So sweetly I kissed you,
   And whispered goodnight . . .'

CLARA lay on her back in the punt and sang,
her bony knees stuck in the air, her blue flannel
knickers showing, her hair in her eyes.

'And nobody missed you
   On your wedding night.'

She sang in a high, adenoidal voice which she
thought was how Americans sang.
   'Armitage.'
   'Stupid.'
   'Bembridge.'
   'Boring.'
   'MacWhitty.'
   'An unpleasant juvenile.'
   'Groby.'
   'A nice child.'
Susan and Wilkins were going through the

photograph. They had reached the second row, but it was taking them a long time.

Sam said: 'Shut up. That song makes me want to pee.'

'Really, the words he learns from that Tom. Hambrake?'

Wilkins thought hard. 'A mouldy pest. Mean with her sweets.'

> 'I came at the sunset
> And left with the dawn . . .'

'Todhunter.'

'A camel-faced paper chewer.'

> 'And then when our lips met . . .'

'Shut up!'

'He's in a bad temper,' Clara said, 'about his poor Tom.'

'Tom isn't poor.'

'How does he get his money, then?'

'He fiddles it. He says so long as the Queen's got a soldier he'll have a pound note.'

'He's ill, anyway. Mummy said so.'

'He's not. He's strong. He's broken the record for the river in a skiff.'

'That was years ago. Do you know what I think now?' Clara lifted her thin brown arms and clasped her hands on the cushions behind her head, looking at Sam with lowered lids. It was a gesture that in the years to come, when it moved breasts under her dress, would be stirring and effective. Now, as she was quite flat chested, had chocolate round her mouth and her hair in her eyes, it was a sort of languorous parody. 'Do you know what I think about Tom?'

'What?'

'I think he'll very soon be dead.'

'He won't,' Sam shouted. 'He won't ever be dead.'

'Yes, he will,' Clara sang. 'Let him die, let him die, God bless him.'

'Obstreperous juveniles,' Susan said. 'Shut up.'

They came to a fork in the river. In the main stream white posts and flags had been erected. There was a white grandstand on the bank, an erection of girders and planks as elaborate as the bleached skeleton of an enormous prehistoric monster. To their left the stream flowed fast under a willow tree down a long backwater.

'There's the regatta course,' Sam said. 'I bet you anything Tom wins the skiff race this year.'

'Are we going to race down the course?'

'No, we're going down the backwater.'

'No, Sam. Susan, stop him.'

But the little boy had stuck in his paddle and twisted the nose of the punt under the willow tree. The stream caught the boat and hurried it between high banks, over gravel where the water was only a foot deep and then under a bridge to where the river was faster and deeper. They were taken past the backs of riverside bungalows let for holidays, bungalows with gardens as dirty and untidy as the strips behind houses glimpsed from a railway train.

'Sam, we're not to go down here. It takes too long.'

'We can't turn round now.'

'Never mind,' Clara said cheerfully. 'Goodbye, home. See you next year.'

In the gardens sad, intimate washing hung over broken tennis nets. A very thin man in an American flying-jacket was fishing, sitting on an upturned bucket. A middle-aged couple, fat, hot, and both with crinkly hair, had taken off their glasses to lie on an uncut lawn with their arms round each other. As the children passed they unclasped and the woman, red in the face, sat up to gaze after them.

'Sam, you know Mummy said not to be too long.'

'She only said that. She won't mind how long.'

'Why not?'

'The man. She's got the man to talk to.'

'He'll have gone by now,' Susan said. 'He's only a tramp.'

'He'll stay for ever. Sleeping in the boathouse.'

A dog ran out of its kennel and barked at them, rearing and pawing the air as it was stopped by the shortness of its chain. As the backwater twisted they came to a boatyard and a man planing a plank stood upright to look after them and spit. Clara's hand, stretched over the side, brushed the reeds with a little sighing noise. There was a sound from someone's wireless and, in the distance, from a railway line. Something floated past Sam in the water, he turned his head away at first and then made himself look.

> 'And over the Rockies
> I rode away
> Into the sunrise
> On your wedding day . . .'

It was a moorhen, dead. It floated flat and heraldic, like a bird painted on a shield. Sam had to push it with the end of his paddle, it went under the water and then rose wet and lifeless.

'Anyway,' he said, 'Tom's not so old.'

The trees closed over the narrow stream and they drifted into the tunnel, green and artificial as a tunnel in a fairground grotto of love. Down this tunnel the girls' voices echoed, chilly and precise.

'Watkin.'

'A lunatic.'

'Mildred Cophammer.'

'A peach . . .'

WHEN she was alone again Julia touched herself, the loose hair at the back of her head, her lips with the tip of her fingers, her neck with her flat hand. This, surely, was by no means her. She avoided the mirror, however, frightened of it.

If something was happening, it was not to her. To Julia Swinton nothing could happen, not death, not disease, not disaster nor unmanageable love. Other people's children died, their husbands ran away, they found themselves in danger, but not her. Then she thought, but if it happens it must happen just like this, on an ordinary day with the children out on the river; ordinary people with no experience to guide them find themselves suddenly, unbearably, confronted with love or death.

She was cold and she wanted to go upstairs and find something to put on. She went into the hall and up the wide, Victorian staircase which had had, as long as she could remember, two stair-rods missing.

On the landing Sam's blazer lay in a limp, inexcusable heap outside the bedroom door. The doors of all the bedrooms were open and a tap dripped in the bathroom.

From the top of the stairs she could see into half of the big bedroom that was used by herself and Swinton. There was a white marble fireplace and beside it a long mirror on a stand. In the mirror she saw the reflection of the man's back.

She held her breath and stepped backwards down one stair. The stair creaked and he came round the door, out on to the landing. He was standing in front of her, looking down at her from the top of the stairs. She was standing insecurely, one foot lower than the other. His hands were swinging at his sides.

Again the moment was endless. Now she only saw his hands and thought of the girl broken and dead at the foot of a flight of stairs, the girl he had told her always looked so fragile. She couldn't speak or move her foot on the steps.

'You thought I'd gone away,' he spoke almost triumphantly. She nodded her head, making no sound.

'I went into the garden and saw the policeman. Then I came into the hall and heard some of what he said. When I thought he was coming out I came up these stairs. Stupid of both of you not to hear me.'

He moved nearer, across the landing and on to the staircase. She was within his reach.

'He's reminded me,' he said, 'what I came here for.'

Whilst he spoke he kept still. She wanted him to speak again. She said: 'What did you do?'

'When?'

'Yesterday. When you saw your sister.'

He was pale, not smiling. 'How much did he know about that?'

'He seemed to know everything.'

'I don't want it talked about. I'm not going to have it talked about.'

'You must.'

'No,' he almost shouted. 'No one's going to know about it. About her.'

'What did you do?'

'Nothing. Keep quiet.'

She turned and ran away from him. As she ran down the stairs she could see the telephone on the hall table. Propped against it was the piece of paper with the telephone number on it. As she picked up the telephone the piece of paper fluttered to the ground. She felt his arm round her waist and his fingers locked on her wrist. She couldn't understand his being so strong.

'You're not going to telephone them.'

Uselessly she tried to pull the mouthpiece towards her. No one spoke from the exchange.

'You're not going to telephone them.'

'I must. He told me to. I must.'

She struggled again. His other arm circled her. In his hand was something bright which caught the rays of light from the glass in the front door.

'You're not going to because of this. I'd have to tell them where I found it if they asked me.'

She looked down at the thing in his hand, her grasp on the telephone slackening as if she were being drugged.

'Where did you get it?'

'Picked it up in the houseboat last night.'

She dropped the telephone and the mouthpiece hung, dead and useless on its cord. His arm round her relaxed. She turned to face him.

'Tell me about it.'

'I was going to. That was what I came to tell you about. Only we got so interested in other things.'

There was a click from the mouthpiece, a small meaningless mutter as the exchange answered. She picked up the telephone and put it back on its rest.

'Come into the sitting-room.'

He followed her and then sat down and put the object on the arm of his chair. It was dull and silver, heavy, Victorian and probably not very valuable, the bottom of a case that could be used for cigarettes; it had a top to slide down over it like a cigar-case. She had given it to Swinton the day they had moved into the house, to commemorate the occasion.

'NOW look what's happened.'

'We're aground.'

At the end of the backwater the punt ran on to a high bank of sand under the water and stuck. Sam pushed his paddle into the sand and tried to use it as a pole, but nothing happened. On each side of them were clumps of rushes, a few yards in front the depths of the main stream. It was very quiet and hot, and they had long ago passed the nearest house. The river smelt sour and bitter, flies buzzed round their bare legs, a black tree root stuck out of the water like the snout of a crocodile.

'On the hills, behind the high grasses, he heard the throbbing of drums. Sam is stuck. Sam is grounded. No more law in the river. Then there was a whistle, and a little twang as the first poison dart, sent from an unseen blowpipe, flew past his ear and stuck into a tree. He felt in the pocket of his bush shirt for tobacco, filled his pipe. For god's sake, he said, get the women out of this.'

'You're all too heavy,' Sam said. 'Someone's got to get out.'

'I will.' Clara kicked off her sandals, pushed her dress into her knickers and got out and stood in the water. She looked down at her feet, strange and white in the water, a piece of weed drifted by and wrapped itself round her calf. There was a black cloud of minnows and she was afraid they would tickle her.

'No good.' Sam heaved on the paddle. Susan took off her shoes and socks and stood beside Clara. Sam, who wasn't wearing shoes, got out and stood beside them. They all pushed the punt. It didn't move.

Wilkins, the visitor, still sat high and dry on the cushions. She saw the family, bare-legged, solemn, strangely similar, regarding her from the water. She knew from the look in their eyes that they were united, with only one thought. Reluctantly she started to unlace her shoes.

When they were all out, the punt floated. They pushed it into the deep water and climbed aboard. When they got moving again all the Swintons sang a song, the words of which Wilkins didn't know.

IT was the passion for putting names on things that was absurd. They had names on their cups, initials on their towels and silver, and on this case she had had his name engraved in full, because he had a habit of losing things, and the address of the house into which they had just moved.

She looked at the case, at the man sitting back in the chair. She could understand nothing now, nothing at all, except that her husband, whom she had seen safely off on the train, had come back into the day as tangibly as if he had come into the room, and he seemed to have joined the man opposite her as something strange, something to be afraid of.

'You see,' he said, 'you can't telephone them now.'

'No. I can't.'

'Don't you want to know some more? Don't you want to know all about it?'

She didn't want to know, above all things, she didn't want to.

'I want to tell you. I've been wanting to tell you
for a long time.'

She felt tired, tired to death and the only thing
she wanted was to go to sleep. Not on the big
double bed upstairs; never on that bed again.

'You know so little. You understand so very
little. I want you to understand everything about
me.'

About him? Why, at this time, should she want
to know about him? She had lost interest in him,
suddenly, completely. She wanted to understand
about herself, about why this should happen to
her who had done, surely, nothing to deserve it.
She thought of the life she had wasted, longing
bitterly to be young and free again, free of the
time which, looking back, she hated. She was like
a religious who, after years of withdrawal and
dedication is convinced, on the brink of middle
age, that God does not exist.

'You know she was my sister?'

'Yes.'

'Can I have a drink?'

Without answering, she heard him go into the
kitchen and come back with two glasses.

'Shall I pour one for you?'

'No.'

He's going to operate on me, she thought, and
he hasn't the courage to do it until he's had a
drink. She waited for him, watching.

'I hadn't seen her since, since that business I told
you of.'

She was only half listening. She had forgotten

the story, it being obliterated by the sight of the cigarette case on the arm of his chair.

'I got there late last night. I'd been walking. I heard that man talk about the boat, but I found it at the landing stage too. I rowed myself over.'

His voice was still precise, but he was talking more quietly, less excitably than before. They were both absorbed in their own stories, which had not yet found a point of contact.

'I went into the houseboat. I'd been there before, you know. There's a kitchen and then a sort of living-room, and then an end room with a stairway up to the roof. The kitchen was much dirtier than yours.

'In the living-room, she hadn't made her bed. She had all sorts of stupid things, little statues and china hands and silly Victorian postcards. There was a big mirror with shells round it, she'd stuck our photograph in its frame. On the bed there was the coat of a man's pyjamas. I thought the room was so horrible I was going away.

'All the same, I went into the end room, to see if she was there. Have you ever seen anyone dead?'

She blinked, as if he had just woken her.

'No. I never have.'

'Neither had I. It's not frightening. She looked, I can't tell you, as though she'd fallen anyhow, like a doll thrown in a corner.

'On my way out I saw this silver thing on a shelf, there were lots of other stupid things, the things she collected, but there was this with his address on. And I thought, I don't hate her any more, but I hate J. F. Swinton of River House.

'So I thought, J. F. Swinton of River House, I'll go and see you and hurt you if I can. I went back in the boat and found the way up here. When I got here I was tired, so I went to sleep in the boathouse because I thought, I'll hurt him better in the morning. In the morning a little boy swam in and looked at me.'

'Sam.' They had both got a quietness, a calm in their voices. She was watching his fingers, turning over the case on the arm of the chair.

'Yes. So I thought, all right, J. F. Swinton, you've got little boys. I'll wait a bit and see what else you've got, dogs, I shouldn't wonder, and a cat and a nice respectable wife who doesn't know anything about all this. When I know everything you've got I'll know how to hurt you badly. I saw him go off to work, you know.'

'Did you?'

'I saw him get into the car without looking at you because he was so sure of everything, and the children fitted nicely into the back. All day you'll be sure of yourself, I thought, and in the evening you'll find it all gone, exploded, because of where I found your cigarette case. He was like my father going off on his rounds.'

Julia frowned, hardly understanding how any-one could hate what had been all her life, but listening, suspecting that she might be learning to hate it too.

'Even then I didn't come out. I learnt as much

as I could about you all before I spoke to you. I
saw that you were beginning to get frightened
and I was pleased because I thought, in the end,
you'd all be frightened, more and more frightened of me, of this.' He lifted the case and let it
fall again on to the arm of the chair.

'I thought I'd stay with you a long time. I
thought I'd make you pay money.'

'Do you want money?'

'No. Take it. It's a free gift.' He threw the case
and it landed in her lap; she closed her fingers on
it, holding it tightly.

'I don't want money. I don't want to be like
him. I don't want to have things with my name
on them.'

'What do you want?'

But he didn't answer her, talking as if she
weren't there, and she looked at him, uncertain if
it was the same man who had started nervously,
unsure of himself, and who had seemed to grow
older as he talked.

'And then, when you first let me into the kitchen, I was puzzled. You didn't want to get rid
of me, you weren't afraid of me any more. You
wanted me there. I thought, perhaps by now she
hates him as much as I do.'

'You were wrong.'

'Yes. I know that too. But then I found out I
wanted to stay here. I liked it. I wanted to be with
you.'

'Why did you show me this?'

'You made me.'

'I didn't make you. I never wanted to see it.'

'Sooner or later you'd have had to know.'

'No, I wouldn't. Never.'

Her clenched hands, clutching the cigarette case, made a little gesture of determination.

'Then I had to tell you. Even when I'd liked you, liked the place, I couldn't have gone away without doing it, I couldn't have been rational and tolerant just to save myself the trouble.'

She looked at him; the room was misty, out of focus, seen through water.

'Why not? Why not leave us alone?'

He stood up and came over to her chair, standing in front of her. He said: 'You have to find out things. Ask questions of everybody. You can't stop finding things out.'

'What's going to happen to us?' Her voice was breaking and her fists struck her knees as she asked him.

'You'll find that out too.'

'Are you going to stay to see him?'

'No. I've told you now. I can't tell him any more.'

Suddenly he was kneeling in front of her, looking at her face.

'I'm going. Are you sorry about that?'

She didn't answer, but she asked him: 'Do you think he killed her?'

When she said it the mist cleared, the room was visible, his face was looking sharply at her.

'I don't know him. You'll find it all out.'

She ran her finger along the case. 'This thing,'

she said, 'had a top. Was it off when you found it?'

He looked downward, as if the question were unexpected. 'I think the top was off when I found it.'

'Was it in her – in the room, do you think?'

'I can't remember. The shelves were covered with little objects. I told you, stupid things.'

'Then the top might still be there?'

'Why? Could anyone tell it was his?'

'Only if they started asking. A lot of people have seen this case. There aren't many like it.'

There was a silence. Then he said: 'I'm going.'

'Yes.' And then, although she couldn't understand why, she asked him: 'Where to?'

'As far as I can. I'll walk up to the main road and see if I can catch a lorry. They give me,' he sounded almost pleased with himself again, as if the trouble were all over, 'long lifts.'

'Someone might see you. I'll take you up in the car.'

'You're very kind to me.'

'Yes.'

He was standing quite still in the room, looking out at the river and the tree, when she went to fetch the car. She started the car and brought it round to the front door. He got in beside her and she told him to sit down low and try not to be seen. Then she drove fast up the lanes behind the house, keeping to the narrow roads that no one used. A man was cutting nettles but he didn't look up. Apart from him they saw nobody. It was very hot. Now and again, between gaps in the hedges, she saw green and gold fields spread out like a map, silent and deserted.

They kept climbing and there was only a purr from the engine and the hiss of gravel under the tyres. Neither of them spoke. Then they drove through a wood and slowed down to where the main road crossed. It was a wide road, straight and fast, which dived down the hill towards a little litter of cafés and petrol stations. He waited until they saw a lorry in the distance, then he opened his door.

'Goodbye,' he said. 'I'm sorry I had to come.'

She didn't answer him and he ran out to the side of the road, waving at the lorry. The lorry stopped and he climbed in beside the driver. The driver slammed the door and waited to light a cigarette. Immediately the man began to talk to the driver, asking, she imagined, questions. The driver threw his match out of the window and the lorry started.

For a little while Julia sat without moving. There was a pause, a silence, before she became involved, as she had to be involved, in the rest of the day. She felt a loneliness so overpowering that it stifled and killed all her other feelings. Now, in all that she had to do, she would be alone. She opened her hand and rubbed the palm gently, thoughtfully against the steering wheel. Then she turned the car and drove it back, through the darkness of the wood.

AT the same time a peace and a stillness had descended on the children. The place they chose to picnic was a small, flat piece of grass by the river; behind it trees of an extraordinary height reached up to the hillside which overhung the water. These trees had narrow, grey pillars of trunks and foliage like hangings. Through them the yellow sunlight was aimed on to the grass like light on to a stage. The place had, indeed an artificial, manufactured appearance, the grass so trim and green, the trees so delicate and carefully placed, that it was like an elaborate open-air theatre in an old palace, and the children might have been posed for an audience seated across the river.

Dwarfed by the trees they sat round a tablecloth which, in an unusual moment of domesticity, Clara had insisted on bringing. They were quite silent and lay on the faded green velvet of the punt cushions, propped on one elbow, eating with one hand, like idle and diminutive Romans.

Sam rubbed the front of his bare feet against

the warm velvet and bit into an apple. He had forgotten everything, the face in the boathouse, the old man at the lock, and he only felt the sun and the cold sour taste of the apple against his teeth.

Clara rolled over on to her stomach and sighed as if her heart were breaking. She had the art of becoming, in a moment, disastrously bored.

'Yes,' she said; 'but what shall we *do*?'

'Act something, why don't you?' Now, far away from the home, Susan had gradually become maternal, caring for them, almost liking them.

'All right.'

Clara jumped to her feet and pushed the food off the tablecloth, running into the trees with the big white thing spread out behind her like a sail.

'Guess what I am when I come out.'

Sam turned round to look at the river. A launch went by and made the moored punt rock like a boat in a high sea. He saw a swan flying, its long neck stretched out. Then, for no reason, he remembered Tom saying that they had done in some tart.

'Clara!' He turned back to look at the trees. 'Clara, come out!'

'She's dressing up. She's all right.'

'Come out, Clara!'

There were shadows round the trunks of the trees.

'Clara, you've got to come out of there!'

The little girl came out with the tablecloth right

over her head and face. Only her thin, bare arms stuck out in front of her, and she walked with exaggerated stiffness, like a sleep-walker or a puppet.

'Clara! Stop it, Clara!'

'Whrrrr!' She made a frightening noise, she was a ghost. Sam ran at her. 'Shut up! You've spoiled it all!'

'Come on, you two. We ought to pack up.'

But Sam was almost crying. 'It's not funny,' he said. 'It's not funny a bit.'

FIRST Julia drove back to the house, and then she took the car out again and drove into the town, past the railway station and over the bridge. She took the road that ran by the side of the river, and stopped the car in the asphalt car park by the bathing place that had been built by the Corporation to add to the amenities of the town. She went in through the gates and bought a ticket from the old woman who sat in the office in a deckchair, knitting.

In the middle of the afternoon on a weekday the bathing place was not crowded. Two boys were throwing a medicine ball, a group of typists on holiday oiled each other's backs and read out each other's horoscopes from a shiny magazine. A fat man lay with the *Daily Mirror* over his face, his stomach hairily rising and falling. In the water were only a few children playing shrilly with a motor tyre, their mothers, shoeless and hot, eyeing them anxiously from the bank. In the beds in front of the changing-rooms the geraniums were pink as bus tickets.

Julia went to the edge of the water and looked across. The island was opposite, only a little way down towards the lock. She could see the white wood of the houseboat under the trees. She had to make herself look.

'Can't see that police boat now.'

Julia could hear the mothers behind her, over the screams from the water.

'Maybe gone off for a cup of something.'

'Charlie, don't drink the water! You don't know what it's got in it.'

'Little devils, aren't they? I expect they've left one over there, don't you? Otherwise, people would be all over it. You know what people are.'

'Pull them trunks up now, Charlie. Of course they're his father's really.'

'Funny how when anything of that sort happens people have to gather round and look at a place.'

'I expect they've left one there. Perhaps the others'll come back with a cup of tea for him.'

Certainly there was no boat moored by the island. She stopped looking and went into one of the changing-rooms.

There, in the darkness that was like the darkness of a cell, she undressed, folding her clothes neatly on a bench. When she was undressed she stood on the duckboards that made the floor of the cell and looked down at herself, at her body pale in the shadows, at her cold, still, feelingless self. It was as if she had been injected with cocaine,

as if she could have stuck pins into her breasts, walked on burning coals, and she would still have felt nothing. Since she had seen the cigarette case the shock had gripped her, dead and hard as an anaesthetic, and she only felt the minutes in front of her, the things she had to do.

If he had just been there when she died, if there was danger for him, for her, for the children, it was clear what she had to do. Only then, when she was naked, looking down at the perspective of her own body, at the breasts which still stood out high and firm, at the stomach which was still flat and at the long line of her thighs, only then did she have the other suspicion, and her body winced as if, in a moment of weakness of the drug, it had felt the pain of the operation.

It was only for a moment and then, with the children shrieking outside, the mothers chattering, the whirr of the lawnmower over the municipal grass, she pulled on her bathing-dress, looked in a piece of tarnished mirror to push her hair under a cap, and walked out into the sun. Until she had done this, she knew, it was no good thinking.

When she was getting into the water a steamer passed, its benches under the white awnings almost empty. There was a man in a checked coat on the deck, drinking beer from a bottle, and he pulled the neck of the bottle out of his mouth to whistle at her. She walked down the steps slowly, sadly, meeting the water quietly as it rose about her.

She swam methodically, with a deliberate and careful breast stroke which they had taught her as a child. She swam up the river, away from the lock, so that no one should see that she was making for the houseboat. When she got opposite the end of the island she was surprised how tired she felt.

She turned over in the water and swam towards the island, swimming behind it so that she couldn't be seen from the bathing place. The bank she was opposite now was flat and deserted, while on the island a curtain of willows hung down to the water. She pushed her way under the willows and she was in a dark passage of water, where the scum of the river and driftwood floated against the broken bank of the island. She stopped swimming and walked on mud, the water covering her breasts.

She went slowly, very quietly, until, over the brambles and tangled laurel, among the trees on the island, she saw the grey Venus looking down on her, peaceful under her stone canopy. It was so quiet that she couldn't believe that there was anyone on the island.

She was still numb, without feeling, so that it was like a dream when she pulled herself out of the water and found herself lying on the grass behind the wall of the miniature temple. She pulled herself to her feet and leant with her back to the wall, her breathing heavy, tireder than she could ever remember being before.

And then, on the other side of the wall, she

heard a footstep. Someone struck a match against the brick, and she heard a hiss as the match was thrown into the river.

It seemed a quarter of an hour before she allowed herself to breathe again. When she moved it was more than ever as if she were asleep, she seemed so light that her feet pushed her from the ground. She couldn't feel the brambles against her legs. She moved along the wall, hugging it, keeping her back to it for protection, her hands feeling the stone.

The wall, again, was infinite, but she was sorry when her hand felt it ending. She had almost crossed the island and when she turned round slowly she could see, through the dense branches, the length of the houseboat and clear grass beyond it. On the grass was a wicker chair and in it a man was sitting, looking out away from her towards the lock. Let him be the only man, she was praying, they've left behind.

He was smoking a pipe, and she could see the blue smoke lifting over the back of his head. Everything that she saw she saw clearly, but it was unreal, remote as if she were looking through the wrong end of a pair of binoculars.

The door was at the end of the houseboat, too far away. Where she stood, the bushes grew up to the walls, masking her and the window, which was only a little farther down. Thoughtfully she moved forwards, stretching out her arm and pulled at the bottom of the window; almost too quickly, as if deceitfully, it swung out towards her. Nothing locked.

Thinking about it afterwards, trying to remember, she had no idea how she got through the window. She hardly felt the wood, the graze on her knee, the cold stone of a sink over which she climbed. She only remembered closing the window quietly, noticing the dirty plates on the table, looking out of the kitchen into the next room which seemed a blaze of light.

There was light in it from the sun, from the river, from the curtainless windows that looked out over the water; it poured over the white walls and on to the unmade bed, so that the whole room was alive, sparkling, absurdly unconnected with mystery or death. The light shone over the tumbled sheets, the red silk lampshade by the bed was reflected in the witch balls and cheap Victorian mirrors, the ridiculous statuettes and shiny photographs on the shelves. On a table in the middle of the room a sheaf of extraordinary, worthless flowers, weeds of every sort, had been stuck into a scarlet and gold pot which might have been won at a fair. By the door was hanging an object of glass which flashed and tinkled. It was a room at the sight of which a child might have clapped its hands, not noticing the prominence of the bed beside which lay a slipper, worn out in the sole and broken at the heel.

Puzzled, as she suddenly felt, uncertain of herself, intrusive, Julia moved into the room. And there, as if it were a piece of herself that had been imported, she saw a glow of silver on the shelf above the bed. In the mass of small, unconnected trophies it would have been a long time before anyone noticed it, but she knew it and she had it in her hand, holding it tightly.

From where she stood she could see now, into the end room. She saw a table with bottles and a portable gramophone. There was a glass on the table and a glass broken on the floor. She saw the foot of a staircase and when she saw it she noticed the silence and the brightness as something fearful. Her terror of the place began.

In the end room another big window showed her the open river and the lock. She could see the end of the island and the wicker chair. It was empty.

She went back into the kitchen, trying not to run. There was no time for the window, and she tried the door. It opened and she pushed herself out sideways, turning the handle quietly behind her. She saw no one and she slithered straight into the river from the side of the houseboat, holding her breath, letting herself sink into the deep water. It closed over her head and as the green darkness came over her she seemed to see the bright room again, to smell the musky, provocative perfume which had hung in it.

She swam as far as she could under the water. When she came up she had swum too far towards the lock and she saw a policeman standing on the bank. He shouted at her, as he had at her children:

'No swimming round here. Keep away from here, please.'

She nodded obediently and swam back towards the bathing place, the silver object hidden in her hand.

The lightness, the obsession with the moment ahead, remained with her as she drove home. She was away from the staircase and the bed, she had done what she wanted. She felt, somehow, almost happy, as if everything were over, concluded, and there would be no need to talk about it again.

It lasted until she went into the house. There she fitted the two parts of the cigarette case together and put it carefully into the pocket of her dress. When she had it there she took it out and looked at it, remembered buying it, ordering the engraving, leaving it, wrapped in a parcel, by his plate at breakfast. She remembered how he had taken her in his arms and she had felt his body against hers, big and hard, his chest against her cheek. It had been the start of their life in the house and now it was a mystery, meaningless, frightful, beyond her power to understand.

Tiredness and misery surged over her. She was lost, left, without anything to do or anyone to guide her. She couldn't think about him and she couldn't think about anything else. They had been together, she and Swinton, on an island, all round was a sea of uncertainty and unknowingness and now it had swept over them. She was drowning, and drowning alone.

She felt the carpet under her knees, her head against the chair he sat in, her hands gripped its arms. The man had said she would have to find it all out, but she wanted to discover nothing, to know nothing but the hearth rug, his chair, that he was coming back to her. As she closed her eyes she again seemed dazzled by the brightness of that other room, the tinkling of the glass deafened her, the perfume choked her and made her feel sick. Violently, uncontrollably, she began to weep.

Far away, over the hills above the river, there was a sound of thunder.

TOM, hearing thunder, looked over to the patch of gun-metal sky above the trees on the hill. He knew it had been too hot to last. On top of it all the weather made his head ache.

'Go home!' he shouted to the children in the punt. 'That sky's coming down in a minute!'

'Tom! Tom, will you go in for the skiff race next year?'

He squatted down beside them, his boots creaking, his shirt dark and wet.

'What you on about?'

'Go in for the skiff race next year. You'd still beat them all.'

I wouldn't, he thought, I'd fold up dead in the bloody boat. 'I might do that,' he said. 'Beat a few of them anyway,' he boasted hopelessly, pleased, somewhere deep inside him, by what the little boy had said. 'Now, go home before you get your breeches wet.'

'Go in for it, Tom. I'll help you train.'

'You do that.' He straightened himself up.

'Lend us the girls' skipping-rope. Keep me off the bloody beer.'

'Right off it,' Sam shouted happily.

The sky was darkening as if a bottle of ink had been spilled across it. A little cold wind ruffled the surface of the river, a duck landing skidded across the water and into the rushes.

Sam said: 'It isn't going to rain.'

But as Tom walked back to his house the sky spat, heavy and contemptuous, on to his boot. When the punt got out of the lock the rain began to fall down on them, thick and warm, pattering on the wood and bouncing off into the swollen river. The children laughed and shouted, as if they were playing under a fountain, screamed and joked like clowns under a toppling bucket of water in the circus. On the bank a woman ran out for her washing, billowing and darkening on a clothes line, the others in the bathing place ran for the changing-rooms, wet, undressed children dancing behind them.

Past the houseboat and the island the punt moved with painful slowness. The launch was back, a curious hood covering the end of it, the men inside talking under cover. The houseboat glimmered through the rain, dead white against the heavy grey of the river, the wet green of the trees.

In the punt Clara had made a tent of the table-cloth, she sat under a shapeless pyramid, wet and laughing. Susan and Wilkins lay under the punt cushions, their heads and feet sticking out, their chins against the velvet that the rain made cold and slimy. Severed from their bodies their heads looked fresh and bright, their cheeks wet with rain, their eyes shining. Sam paddled slowly and deliberately, the rain plastered down his hair so that he looked like a small water animal. It ran down his neck and under his arms and into his shoes. When he felt the raindrops on his skin, moving down his cheeks cold and wet, he thought they were drops of blood and that he was wounded in the head and struggling on, bleeding like a pig.

Other children, dry in a boathouse on the bank, laughed at them and pointed. They were isolated under the rain in the middle of the grey river. At last, when Sam's clothes were black and heavy, his shoes full of water, they got to their own boat-house. They carried in the cushions and stood in the dining-room, dripping. Julia came in to them; her eyes were dry, she had no more tears left.

THE train, returning from London, had few passengers by the time it reached the town. They got out one by one, Swinton last so that he walked alone up the length of the platform. He passed the barrier and stood in the entrance of the station looking out at the rain. Three hearse-like taxis stood in line against the pavement opposite, in the window of the railway café a naked electric light bulb was burning over piles of dummy cigarette cartons, an old woman stood in the rain with a sack over her shoulders selling papers. The town, which had looked in the morning as if it were brightly painted scenery, now looked drab and small and grey.

Swinton waited, found a packet of cigarettes and lit one, throwing the match into the gutter. Then he crossed the road to a taxi, moving slowly, hardly noticing the rain, and as if he were uncertain. In the first taxi the driver was asleep at the wheel, his head down and his neck outstretched like the neck of an old, brooding horse.

The inside of the taxi was large and grey and uninviting, like a damp sitting-room. Swinton avoided it, telling himself that he was cold, that he needed a drink.

He walked up the glistening stone steps, through the yellow Gothic doors of the Railway Arms. On one side of the entrance hall was the dark public bar in which two porters stood drinking stout. On the other was the saloon and Swinton was out of the rain into the glare of unshaded light bulbs. He also came into a sudden silence and faces turned to look at him.

In fact there was only a small blaze of light behind the bar which gave it a mechanical cheerfulness, like a Christmas tree lit up against the dark entrance of a suburban church. There were three strips of light behind the bottles which glowed unnaturally and made the drink inside appear vivid and unsafe. There was a standard lamp fixed into a pink glass elephant and a row of coloured bulbs over the glasses. This illumination shone in the earrings of the manageress and made highlights and deep shadows across the bosom of her red silk dress.

'Good evening, sir. What can I get you?'

She was looking at him with small eyes as bright and artificial as her earrings. The other men in the bar were silent, as if interrupted in a conversation and unable to think of anything different to say.

'Beer, please.' Swinton was thirsty.

'Yes, sir. Paint or half-paint?' The manageress

was refined. Farther up the bar one of the men said: 'Must push along now. Supper, you know. Can't risk umbrage again tonight.'

'Just half.'

Another voice said: 'What surprises me is they've kept it out of the papers.'

'Terrible out, isn't it, sir?'

The manageress was standing opposite Swinton with his beer. When he had paid her without answering she drifted back along the bar like a hostess at a party who, having done her duty with a dull guest, is getting back to her friends.

'No, but, George, they always keep it out until the police are certain, that's rait, Mr Durmwurm, isn't it?'

She was leaning across the bar, her breasts pillowed on her folded arms, and talking so quietly that Swinton could hardly hear what she said. The name, for instance, was a meaningless buzz of sound.

'In my experience of the force, Mrs Martin, yes. It may mean they haven't finished their' – a pause like a politician's, a soupy, reassuring, deep voice, no doubt Mr Durmwurm – 'their inquiries.'

'They were saying in the shop today,' a new, high, excited voice, 'that they're looking for someone who was over there with her last night.'

'I should think there was someone with her every night, wasn't there? One for the road now, Mrs Martin. Great umbrage if I don't go now.'

'Really, George. Why don't you telephone, dear?'

'I did. Half an hour ago. To say I'd be back in five minutes. People in to dinner, you know. Soup cold and all that. Frightfully difficult.'

'If someone was over there last night,' Durmwurm again, 'they shouldn't take long to find out who it was.'

Swinton raised his head slowly from his glass like an old and experienced soldier delicately taking observation. Again he thought they were all silent and all looking at him, again the manageress was the only one to break the silence.

'Another, sir?'

'Yes. Yes, the same again, thank you.' He had to stay and listen, but he turned his eyes away from them, stared at a mechanical fortune-telling device on the bar. For a penny a pointer swung round the printed labels foretelling the future. Swinton didn't try it. He could see the faces of the three men reflected in the glass.

Durmwurm was on a bar stool, a retired man about the town, with a white moustache stained with nicotine, a high stiff collar and lemon-yellow gloves. The man anxious to be home, a plump man in an open camelhair coat, the whites of whose eyes were red from too many for the road, was standing with one hand in his pocket, the other clutching a pink gin. The third man, pleased to be with them, was the manager of the wireless shop, young and enthusiastic, with protruding teeth and a row of pencils and fountain pens in the breast pocket of his jacket.

Again the manageress gave Swinton his drink quickly and again she walked back to the end of the bar.

'Who could it have been, though? She didn't know many people in the town.'

'Hardly anyone. I fixed her portable for her once. Curious old box. Made a noise like a train.'

'She once stopped the car to ask me the way. Joan came up when we were talking. Terrific umbrage.'

'Looked underfed to me. But you couldn't help noticing her.'

'I always said she never really joined in, not even when she came here for a drink. Not like one of us. Do you really think it was just an accident?'

'It could have been.' The voice from the bar stool was rich and contemplative. 'It could have been. All I can say is, the police have been over there a long time.'

'I can't think of anyone she knew particularly.' The manageress sounded thoughtful. 'Not just rait off, I can't. I wonder who it was they think was with her.'

'Mr Swinton.'

The voice came from behind Swinton, from the door. When he heard it his mouth set and a muscle in his jaw quivered. He put down his drink and, with the bar door open, he was suddenly very cold.

'Mr Swinton, fancy meeting you. Such trouble all day.'

Swinton turned round slowly. Lorwood was wearing a mackintosh and a cloth cap, and carrying a string bag in which there were two empty beer bottles.

'Refills, please, Mrs Martin. Perhaps you'd put a small whisky in this medicine bottle, would you? My sister's not well. On your way home, Mr Swinton?'

'Yes. Tell me,' Swinton tried to speak very quietly, only looking at the old, smiling face under the cap, feeling that everybody else was listening. 'Tell me. What's happened?'

'Surely you've heard. Miss Paneth in the house-boat, she had some sort of an accident.'

'She's dead?'

'Why, yes. Yes, she is. Is it in the paper?'

Now he knew that they were listening, thinking over every word. He had to be careful.

'No. I don't believe it is.'

'It's been an anxious day. A policeman came and I believe that upset my sister. After he'd gone she had a really very ugly go of tummy. Had to be put to bed.'

'I'm sorry.' Swinton still spoke quietly, choosing every word. 'I knew nothing about it.'

'I had the quack in naturally. Nothing he could do for her. Thank you, Mrs Martin, and a small gin for me.' Lorwood stowed away the bottles, suddenly looking cheerful. 'Of course she's seventy years eleven months and she does all the heavy work in the house. It's killing her, slowly killing her.'

'Do you know when this accident happened?'

'Oh, last night. I know that. I mean that's what they said. No one knows what to think.'

Lorwood raised his gin. He was looking at Swinton and smiling.

Swinton said: 'Do they know how it happened?'

'Just falling down some steps, I believe. There's only some conundrum about her boat.'

'Her boat?'

'They found it this morning, tied up by the towpath. It was the only way she had of getting across the river.'

The man on the bar stool interrupted them, speaking directly to Swinton for the first time.

He wanted to go then, to walk as quickly as he could away from them and out into the rain. But he didn't move. He saw their eyes, the watery eyes of two men and a third whose eyes were concealed by glasses, the shining eyes of the manageress and the secret laughing eyes of Lorwood.

He said: 'Then it's a mystery.'

'If you're taking a taxi,' Lorwood said, 'might I join you?'

'I'm afraid I must make a call first.'

'Tonight?'

'I'm afraid so.'

'Good evening, then. I expect Mrs Swinton

will have something to tell you about the day's excitement. Remember me to her.'

'Yes.'

'You know it's a foolish thing, but I always test the future on this machine.' Lorwood took out a penny and put it into the slot. The arrow circulated into a little whirl and then came to rest by a label. Lorwood peered down to read it. 'Your next will be a boy! Absurd. Why does one yield to these things?'

He turned round to speak to Swinton, but Swinton had gone. The door of the saloon bar was still swinging. The manageress said: 'He never finished his drink.'

The street was empty. There were no faces, no sounds except the rain in the gutter. He walked fast and didn't feel the rain. Even the taxis were gone. He was alone in the town.

The streets were sweating and slippery. The shops closed and barred. Swinton walked close to them, his hands in his pockets, his coat collar turned up. Two hours before he had been arguing with a foreman in a workshop alive, vibrating with machinery. In two hours' time he would be at home with Julia. Now he was alone, in a town that had changed. The streets were dangerous. He wanted to get out of them.

In the centre of town the traffic lights changed colour, red and green pointlessly, no cars stopped or started. Down the High Street to the bridge, the teashops, chemists, photographers, had grilles across their doors like prisons. In the photographers' windows shapeless brides and embarrassed grooms grinned at him. On the church tower the clock struck again and again, splitting the silence. It wasn't far to the bridge and the river. He wanted to be away from the streets, near to the river.

He walked faster when he saw a policeman in a doorway, the rain dripping from his cape. The man had seen him and said: 'Goodnight.' Swinton didn't answer. How many people could have seen him that first hot evening? Then the streets were full of children and their mothers, young men on the corners, in open-necked shirts, waited for girls. They could all have seen him, and the three men in the bar could have seen him, looking out of the open windows of the Railway Arms. It was part of his life that only strangers knew about.

In two hours, with Julia, he would talk about the children; Susan's sudden tempers, Clara's mysterious tears. Two hours before he was the boss, too particular about the quality of the wood, with not much patience and no private life. Now he was walking endlessly across the bridge, the wide, pale, swollen river stretched out on either side of him. And all because, one morning in the train, he had offered to light a girl's cigarette.

Anyone could have seen him. Below the bridge he saw the cropped willows, the shadowy tow-path that led past the island to his home. Anyone could have seen him walking there. There had been men fishing, men and girls pushing their bicycles, children paddling.

He came slowly down the steps from the bridge on to the towpath. He walked a hundred yards and only heard his own feet on the gravel, the rain falling and the rustle as some small, unidentified animal slid out of the rushes and into the water. He stopped and made a shelter of his coat collar to light another cigarette. He looked up, dazzled for a moment, by the match. Now he could see the green bulk of trees on the island and the stone Venus placed like the figurehead on the prow of a ship. He couldn't believe she was dead.

The time had been so short. It had only been the moment one morning two weeks before in the hot, dusty railway carriage on his way to work. When he had left home Julia had kissed him remotely, her eye on Sam. The children had been glad, on the whole, to have him out of the house. He sat in the train and read the paper; round the corner of it he saw this girl with an unlit cigarette. He leant forward with a match. He was stung suddenly, not only with desire but with bitterness and regret. It lasted for a moment with the agony of a wound while the sun poured in through the dirty window.

When he saw her afterwards it was to discover that feeling again or kill it. But he had never felt the same until now, when he saw the island in the rain and remembered that they had found her dead there and broken, unnecessarily killed. He thought of her dead and he was steadied, calmed by a new anger. He was angry with the men speculating in the bar, at himself hurrying through the streets. He walked in the middle of the path, deliberately towards the island. It was unimportant who had seen him.

In the train he had thought that he might be about to become old and wanted something to stop it. On the towpath he knew nothing could stop it. But whatever he had learnt there was no reason for her to be dead.

He came opposite the island, the houseboat was on the other side, hidden from him by the trees, and there was no boat at the island. He was near to the landing-stage where he had, when he came this way before, found the boat. The platform was hidden by rushes and the sound of the rain stopped him hearing the low voices.

He stopped by the landing-stage and he saw two men looking at him curiously, one with a thin moustache and a mackintosh, the rain dripping off his hat, the other in a blue uniform with a flat cap. The meeting was unexpected, the two men were standing on the low wooden platform and might have appeared, without explanation, from the water to bar the way to the island. No one spoke. Swinton stood above them on the path and looked across the water, a big man who had come up on them silently, unprotected against the weather. He was gone before they thought of challenging or questioning him, walking quickly again along the side of the river, in the direction of his home.

AGAIN, with something to do, the pain and the fear had receded. Julia had worked until she had the fire alight in the sitting-room, damp logs from the boathouse hissing on it, more logs ranged round to dry. Susan and Wilkins, in dry clothes, lay on their stomachs in front of it reading old fashion magazines, quiet, almost unobtrusive. Clara and Sam, bathed, in dressing-gowns and pyjamas, sat at a table playing whist and eating bananas. In the kitchen she had the supper ready on the table, two bottles of beer cooling in the refrigerator, gin and vermouth on a tray by the fire in the sitting-room, everything got ready, carefully planned as if it were Christmas or a birthday.

It was all done and she was unoccupied. Standing alone in the kitchen, waiting, not knowing what she was waiting for, she could hear the sound of the fire, Sam and Clara quarrelling gently over the cards.

Then the kitchen door handle turned and rattled. This time she wanted to fling herself against it, to bar his entrance. But she stood still.

He came in and shook himself like a dog. His greying hair was wet and ruffled. He took off his jacket and his shirt was dark over the shoulders where the rain had soaked through. First of all, by force of habit, she was sorry he was wet.

'Hallo, darling. I should have rung you. The taxis were all gone. I had to walk back along the river.'

'Why didn't you ring?'

She saw his face, smiling automatically, his eyes remote. Suddenly, with horror, she thought it was all false, not only tonight but all the other nights when he had come home smiling at her, pretending that it was her he had been thinking about all day.

'I thought the rain wouldn't last. Everything all right?'

'Yes.'

'Children enjoyed themselves?'

'I think so.'

'And the one with a name like a hospital nurse, the one you dreaded?'

She found herself retreating from him, into a corner of the room. She didn't want him near or to touch her. And there was an enormous temptation to say nothing, to leave well alone and let the day return, if it could, to normal.

'She's not so frightening.'

'Fine. Shall we have a drink?'

'I'll get it.'

She moved across the room and as she came near him he put out his hands to touch her. It was as if it were a charm, something strong and potent to ward him off, that she found the cigarette case in the pocket of her dress and threw it on to the kitchen table where it clattered and lay still.

'I found that.'

He looked down at it unsurprised, not yet touched.

'Where?'

'In Molly Paneth's houseboat.' The words came out of her quickly tumbled together, she had been waiting to say this to him, and now silent and frightened and a long way away she heard her own voice clattering, almost screaming the story she had held in herself all the afternoon.

'She was killed last night. A beautiful girl everyone tells me. Only your case was there, left in her bedroom. I had to swim over when the police weren't watching and steal it away.'

He was looking at her without understanding either her words or the case on the table.

'Her brother came and gave me half the case. I think he came to blackmail you. He told me she was dead. They all think someone killed her. So I swam over for you. To get the other half. Take it. For god's sake take it and put it away.'

She snatched up the case. She wanted to throw it anywhere, at him, out of the room. She felt a pain in her wrist and looked down. She saw that he was holding her. Her wrist was locked by a big, workman's hand. She thought, a hand like that would break anything fragile.

She had no more words. The ones she had spoken still hung in the air like smoke. She could hear the rain outside running down the gutters of the roof. The walls of the kitchen seemed to be closing in round her, she wanted to break through them and run into the air.

He said: 'Why did you go?'

'I don't know. Why did you?'

When she had thrown down the case she hadn't known exactly what he would do. She had expected him to retreat from her suddenly, to become powerless, or to take her in his arms and ask her to forgive him. But she still felt the pain on her wrist and she realized with bewilderment that he was angry. She couldn't understand him and she knew that she was afraid.

'Julia,' he said. 'What did you think?'

'When?'

'When you found the case?'

She couldn't answer. He was holding her and they were very close but she felt she was seeing him for the first time, like a stranger. The years of days and nights, days when they had drunk together over restaurant tables, nights when their bodies had locked together in bed, the quarrels that had ended when he had kissed the tears from her cheeks, were obliterated, washed out by the rising tide of his extraordinary strangeness and anger.

'What did you think I'd done?'

She could only look at him, at his eyes that were trapped and angry, at his clenched hands and wet shirt and the drops of rain glistening on his hair and his forehead.

She felt her wrist freed and she moved back from him. He said: 'You know I love you.'

She didn't doubt it; it didn't matter.

They had lived together so long and it was so long since she had seen him out of control or in trouble. She still couldn't recognize him as he turned away from her and put on his coat again, automatically feeling in his pocket for the cigarette case that was still on the table. She had loved him too, and would have tried to do so again, to put her arms round him, bury her face in his coat, screw up her eyes until she could see and think of nothing but him, only it was difficult. They had so far to go.

It might have happened even then only he started talking again, in a dead voice she didn't recognize. First it was the same question again.

'Tell me what you thought?'

'Nothing. I thought nothing.'

'When did you first hear about her . . . about it?'

'Campbell said something this morning. At the station.'

'Campbell? Then you said her brother came.'

'Yes.' He was no longer angry but inquisitive and remote. She sat back against the edge of the table. She saw his face pale and set and his voice came from a long way away as if he were shouting down a tunnel. It might still be all right if only he could stop talking, stop asking questions.

'Julia, I must know everything. You must tell me.'

'Go away. Leave me alone.'

She heard herself speaking to him. She realized she was crying. She spoke but it didn't stop him. She saw his face blurred by her tears.

'Has he gone now?'

She nodded.

'Where is he?'

'I don't know. I don't know anything. Stop asking me things. I won't talk about her.'

'Have you seen anyone else. The police?'

'Leave me alone.'

'In a minute. They must have come here. Did they ask about me?'

'You? No.' Her hands covered her face so that she couldn't see him. In the darkness everything was quieter, his questions had the aimless purposefulness of a drunk man in a distant part of the house stumbling to find his way in a dark room.

'Julia, I must go out again. I'll come back when I know it all. Just tell me, did the policeman talk about her boat?'

She couldn't remember, she couldn't tell him. She waited for him to go.

She heard him cross the room and go over to the door. Before he went he said something else, not a question but a statement of fact.

'You think I killed her.'

She heard the door close. His footsteps going away.

She uncovered her eyes then and found that they were dry. She went out of the kitchen and into the hall but he had gone and shut the front door behind him. She found his raincoat still hanging in the hall and took it with her and opened the front door. She looked out, holding the coat in her arms but the garden was wet and empty and she couldn't see him. Then she shut the door carefully and went back into the kitchen.

Susan came into the kitchen and looked at her inquiringly, almost with hope.

'WAS that him?'

'Yes.'

'Has he gone away?'

'Only for a little while.'

'Where is he gone?'

'He didn't say.'

'Oh.'

Susan came and sat friendlily on the edge of the table. Only for a little while, she smiled, an unlikely story. She was not in love with Swinton and dreamt of the day when this curious, inexplicable, sensual partnership which ruled the house would be broken; when her mother would be old and alone and would rely on her for cups of tea, and putting the children to bed.

'Can I help you at all?'

'No. We'd better put the children to bed and then have supper.'

'Without him?'

'Yes.'

It was what she liked, she could talk endlessly

without seeing her father's eyes signalling to her
mother.

'Will you help me cut out my dress?'

'Really, darling, I'm awfully tired.'

Julia was looking out of the window, at the rain
soaking into the grass, hiding the shape of the
monkey-puzzle tree.

'He's often out in the evenings now, isn't he?'

'Susan, that's nonsense.'

'Well, one or two evenings lately.'

'Only when he has to catch a later train. He has
a late meeting at the works or something.'

'Oh, is that it?'

Susan opened the refrigerator door and looked
in.

'We shan't need this beer now, shall we? I say,
shall I make some cocoa for all of us?'

'If you like.'

'I've decided I'm not going to marry. We've
talked it over at school and none of us are.'

Julia, thinking about Swinton, looked at this
large, aloof and unyielding girl, vaguely remembering the solemn and minute baby she had once
held in her arms.

'There's one girl at school whose parents are
divorced and married again. Apparently it's absolutely marvellous, she has a birthday and a Christmas with each one.'

'Does she?'

'Yes, and the step ones are much kinder than
the real ones, so she says. It's awfully amusing
because everything she says to her mother about

her father gets written down and sent to the solic-
itors.'

'Come on, Susan. We'll put them to bed now.'

'Sure you wouldn't like to rest? If you've got a
headache I'll lend you the lavender water I bought
for Wilkins's birthday.'

'No, it's all right, really. I'll come.'

Sam and Clara were tired, they had quarrelled
finally and the cards were strewn on to the floor.
When she had them in bed she leant over Sam and
kissed him, he had his arms up and locked them
round her neck.

'Tell me,' he said. 'How old do you have to be
to die.'

'Oh, very old.'

'Ninety-four?'

'About that.'

'Tom should be all right then, I mean for the
race next year.'

'Quite all right.'

'Really. I mean, he's not much older than you.'

THEY had all gone, the party was over and Campbell, suddenly depressed, didn't feel like washing up the glasses. They stood round the cabin, on the gramophone, on the lockers, even on the glossy covers of his magazines, empty but for a flake of lemon or a half-nibbled olive, making rings with their sticky bases. There were cigarette ends on the floor too, but he didn't pick them up.

It was hot and airless in the cabin, although the rain was drumming on the roof of the launch and sliding heavily across the glass of the porthole. He undid the silk scarf from his neck and wiped the sweat off his face. Then he found a bottle of whisky in a locker and poured himself one straight.

They came suddenly and drank his drink. Old friends from the river like Doreen and Peter who remembered the great days of Maidenhead, new friends like the bank manager's eighteen-year-old daughter whose bust had been the talk of two regattas and who refused to dance with him because, among his records, there was no New Orleans. They came and stood about in sweaters and canvas trousers while he mixed them Old Fashioned and Manhattans or Daiquiris with real Cuban rum. And when they had drunk a little too much they left suddenly because they were going to dinner at Skindles, or because a young man in an Edwardian suit had arrived in a vintage Bentley. And when they had gone, except for the mess, they might never have been there at all.

This was a drink he wasn't going to mix. He poured himself another whisky and felt cooler, more remote. The cabin was bright with glossy wood and chromium and painted plaster galleons on the wall, cheerful as a little corner of Perivale cut out and suspended over the dark water, moored beside the rain-soaked trees.

As he finished his drink he caught sight of his face reflected in an octagonal rimless mirror. A large, shapeless face in misty glasses with shining highlights on his nose and forehead. He wondered vaguely why he looked like that, he had been fat since his schooldays, but he always felt there was a lean, energetic and handsome man somehow imprisoned inside him.

He took another drink. If they didn't like him, then he didn't like them all that much. The bank manager's daughter, in any case, had disappointing ankles. There were his real friends in the signed, framed photographs round the walls, old troupers he had known all his life, Ted, Kenneth,

Ray in dinner-jackets with toothy grins, Iris, Elsie, Pat in low-cut evening-dresses seen through a milky haze. They had all signed their names in large scrawls as if their names were all they had ever learnt to write. They were his friends.

And his friends were the fans who wrote to him after his programmes, signed with love from five girls in the Flodden Motorworks Canteen, two lance-corporals in Dortmund, all in Ward B, Micklehurst County Hospital. He answered all the letters himself. God, how they loved him.

Another drink and he felt even cooler, more handsome, even debonair. The thin man was fighting his way out. Now he remembered it, Julia Swinton had never turned up, he wondered why that was. At the station, he thought, she seemed more forthcoming than usual, even as if she had wanted him to come home with her. A woman like that was worth twenty bank managers' daughters whose figures gave you ideas above their heads. Campbell looked up, he thought he heard a footstep on the deck. He finished his drink quickly and looked round again at the photographs on the wall. They were evenly spaced except for one gap, a place where the panelling showed a lighter square, a patch the same size as the other frames.

He was right. There was someone coming down into the cabin. He pushed back a strand of hair and knotted his scarf round his neck.

'Hallo, I'd given you up. Come in. I say, old man, you are wet. Got Julia in tow?'

Swinton came in slowly, blinking at the light in the cabin.

'No. I'm alone.'

'Oh . . . oh, well, never mind. I'm afraid the party's over, but you'll have a drink?'

Campbell was depressed again. Swinton, he thought, was one of those pleasure haters who never listened to the quiz programmes. It was difficult to think of anything to say to him.

'Children keeping Julia?'

Swinton was looking round at the photographs on the walls, and at the empty space.

'I said I suppose the kids are keeping Julia in.'

'Yes. I'm sorry. Yes. That's it.'

He was still looking at the space on the wall, seeming, Campbell thought, to have something on his mind. Could Julia have said anything to him; anything like, look darling, I'm in love with Campbell. After all, why not? It had happened, not for a few years perhaps, but it had happened. The interviews that followed were flattering but awkward. Best to try a carefully placed red herring.

'You missed a lot of fun. Had young Betty Abbot here, you know, the bank manager's daughter. Wonderful figure. She seems to have a bit of a crush on me. Embarrassing, really.'

'Have you heard about Molly Paneth?'

'Funny how these girls get when it's anyone with a name.' Campbell seemed not to have heard. He took Swinton's glass and refilled it, refilled his own. But without Swinton having to repeat his question Campbell answered it.

'Yes. We were talking about that before you came actually. Tragic business.' His voice was as automatically reverent as a hired morning-coat at a funeral. Swinton said nothing, still looking at the patch on the wall. He wasn't drinking.

Campbell said: 'You knew her, didn't you?'

'I met her once or twice.'

Campbell crossed the cabin and switched on a wireless fitted into the panelling. From far away came the mute, hysterical slidings of a jazz trumpet. He started to smoke, with difficulty bringing the lighted match to the end of his cigarette.

'Had you seen her lately?' Swinton spoke from behind him.

'Not for months. Had you?'

'Yes.'

'Then perhaps you know more about it than I do.'

'I doubt it.'

'Look, what the hell . . .'

Campbell swung round. Swinton was turning over the pile of magazines on top of the lockers.

'Leave them alone, Swinton.'

Under the last one Swinton found a photograph without a frame. He turned it over and the two men looked down at the girl's face, a face unlike all the others on the walls, marked by no cheerfulness but with a look of deep, bewildered, almost terrified happiness.

'What the devil? What do you mean by searching about in here? What are you after?'

'You hid her photograph?'

Campbell's eyes were small and angry. The sweat shone on his nose. He moved clumsily towards Swinton and then, changing his mind, took off his glasses and started to polish them, staring down at the photograph. The tone of reverence returned to his voice.

'Yes. Somehow it didn't seem right to have her on the wall after that happened. She looks happy there, doesn't she? Probably just met some awful type and fallen in love. She was always doing that.'

'I believe she was.'

'Well, it's happened. She's got no worries now anyway.' Campbell put back his glasses, crossed the cabin to the drinks tray and turned the whisky bottle upside down ruefully.

'One for the road? Just a minute, I'll get another bottle. A bottle of the best, like I don't let get seen at parties. Got it among the stores.'

Campbell walked unsteadily out of the cabin door. When he was gone Swinton folded the photograph quickly and put it in the inside pocket of his coat. Swinton was moving slowly, unhappily, towards the discovery he had to make. When he knew the truth he could take it home with him. He wanted to go there soon. He was suddenly tired and sat on an upholstered bench that ran round the cabin.

'Here we are. Bourbon. Have you seen that in England before?'

'Yes. In her houseboat.'

'Really? I've never been there as far as I can remember.' Campbell spoke casually, pouring the drinks.

'That's untrue.'

Campbell put down the bottle and turned round. Again he seemed to be about to make an attack, but again he changed his mind, swallowing the neat whisky from the bottom of his tumbler.

'All right, Swinton. Suppose it is untrue and I have been there. Naturally there are a few things one likes to be – well, reticent about. You've been over there too?'

'Yes.'

'Julia knows about that?'

'She does now.'

'So there's trouble, eh? Bad luck, old man. Very bad luck.'

Campbell laughed. Swinton's hands curved round the edge of his seat, gripping it tightly.

'You must have been the latest then,' Campbell said. 'I only saw her a couple of times this summer. I date much further back, you know.'

Campbell brought his whisky glass over and sat in a basket chair, his stomach distended over the belt of his flannel trousers, his glass resting on his thigh, the chair cracking as he moved. The cabin rocked gently as he looked at it through a haze of alcohol. He arrived, unwisely, at the moment of confidence, seeing the man opposite him as an audience, a grey-haired novice whom he would be pleased to instruct. Outside the rain beat on the porthole insistently, below them the river slapped the sides of the boat.

'In fact, I suppose I was one of the first. I was in an agency in those days. Promised to get Molly a part. As a matter of fact I really could have got her one, I had a play to cast.'

The memory seemed to return to Campbell like the taste of a delicious meal. Swinton got up, walked across the cabin towards him.

'You know the old joke of the casting couch, mostly it's just a gag, but with Molly it worked all right. She seemed quite prepared for it. She was a good girl, afterwards I don't think she bore any malice.'

'Don't you?'

'Of course.' His thick finger circled the rim of his glass thoughtfully. 'Perhaps I never got to know her as well as you. I told you I didn't see her much lately.'

'You were with her last night.'

A stranger peering through the porthole, watching the two men without hearing them, as he might watch the silent, underwater creatures in an aquarium, would have seen the moments of violence occur with a curious slowness, almost like a ritual. The glass of whisky toppling and falling unsupported to the ground. Campbell on his feet, Swinton with his hand flat on the other man's chest forcing him back into his chair.

'What are you talking about?'

'She was with you. Her boat was never taken across. She met you somewhere and you brought her home in your boat. You were together some-time on the island and then you left again in your own boat.'

'What makes you think all that?' He moved in his chair, feeling in his pocket for another ciga-rette.

'She told me she was going to meet you last night. I said I couldn't see her again and she said she was going to meet you. It's very simple.'

Campbell struck a match, looking up at the other man over the flame.

'You are a bloody liar.'

'No.' Swinton shook his head. 'That's how it happened.'

The flame died. The eyes above it looked out desperately as if searching for help in the corners of the cabin. The face shone all over with sweat. The voice went up in pitch, becoming high and querulous.

'Look, Swinton. We're men of the world. Nothing that happened last night was my fault, I swear that. Neither of us come very well out of this business, you know. You go home to your wife now, eh, and we'll forget the whole thing? Sort of thing neither of us would care to be involved in. Don't you see that?'

'We're involved, Campbell. We can't help it.'

'Poor old Mol. No one can help her now. Per-haps she's better off. We've got lives to live. A secret, eh, old man, a secret between us two? Mum's the word, eh?'

The appalling thing, which made the scene more than ever like a dream, was that he was getting drunker, the floor of the cabin slanted up towards him as he spoke and he began, meaninglessly, to laugh. He rose to his feet again, his finger to his lips.

'Dead silence, old man. Silent as the grave.'

'Get out, will you? We've got to start this thing up.'

Swinton had the door open and the rain, blown by a sudden gust of wind spattered the cabin. As the man lurched towards him, he pushed him up the steps, into the open cockpit of the launch. Swinton untied the ropes. Campbell clutched the wheel, the rain blinding him, soaking his shirt.

'Get it started.'

'What's the idea, old man? Where you going?'

'Home. To my home. Up the river. Do as I say.'

Campbell was sobering, wet and frightened. He started the engine, the lights in the cabin dimmed. He turned the wheel clumsily and the boat bumped away from the bank; in the cabin another glass fell to the floor.

As they moved into the centre of the river, Campbell again tentatively spoke, looked round at Swinton.

'I'll take you home certainly. After that . . . You don't want to do me any harm over this, do you?'

Swinton said nothing. His face in the green steering light was pale. He ran his fingers along his forehead as if it were aching.

At last he said:

'I don't want to do anyone any harm.'

SUSAN crossed her bedroom, pulled back the curtains and looked out of her window. In the bright box-like room behind her, with its cretonne bedcover and frilled dressing-table, were the possessions which made up her life, school photographs, Swinton and Julia gazing at each other from each side of a morocco folder, a bloodstained crucifixion left over from a now-dying phase of High Anglicanism. In front of her was the darkness, the wet garden, the river and the rain. She could see the light of the sitting-room window, the room in which she had left her mother alone. It was the first night of a new year, the year that her father left.

At the bottom of the garden she could see the river and she screwed her eyes and leant out farther as the light of a boat came up it. Then the boat stopped. A lamp was switched on and a long beam of light fingered through the rain and the darkness to the back door and to the sitting-room window. Another lamp was switched on on the deck.

Then she sighed, half-disappointed, half-relieved. The changes she had longed for, and yet been a little afraid of, were not to take place. He was back. Everything was going to go on the same. The excitement was over.

He was standing on the deck of the boat. In his hand he had something like a paper or a photograph. Suddenly, with a quick gesture, he threw it into the darkness of the river. Then Susan heard him call out:

'Julia. Julia. Can you come out, darling?'

There was a long silence. Then the back door opened, letting a wedge of light on to the lawn.

'What is it?'

'We're on the launch. Campbell's here. He wants to tell you something.'

Susan leant out farther, she saw her mother's white dress moving out into the garden. Although it was raining, she seemed to be moving very slowly.

'This way. It won't take a minute.'

Julia crossed the lawn and Swinton put out his hand to help her on to the launch. They went down into the cabin and the deck lights were switched out. Susan could only see the light in the cabin. They were having a party, a pleasure for which, Susan always felt, they were far too old.

She went to bed, switched out her light and pulled the bedclothes up to her ears. It was all going to be the same as ever, tomorrow it would all be the same.

'WHAT is it? Why am I to come here?'

Julia looked round the hideous cabin, at the broken glasses and cigarette ends trodden in to the floor, at her husband standing by the door and Campbell back in the middle of the room, sitting in the basket-chair. It was unbelievable, this bright, unnatural room drawn up suddenly at the end of the garden, into which he had invited her to walk.

She looked at Swinton and slowly, although what he was doing was incredible, she recognized him again. He was strange, but not altogether a stranger.

'I'm sorry to bring you here. I wanted Campbell to tell you what happened.'

'What happened when?'

'Yesterday evening, in the houseboat.'

She raised her hand and let it fall against her side, a little gesture of uncomprehending resignation.

Swinton said: 'Tell us, Campbell.'

'Really. I don't see why you have to drag Julia . . .'

He looked at her beseechingly. Julia realized that they were all suffering and yet she was sorry for no one, not even herself.

'Tell us. Then we shall know.'

'It's a sickening business. I don't want to remember . . .'

Swinton went over to the cupboard, poured him a whisky and put it into his hand.

'Tell us. Then it'll be over.'

'All right if you must have it.' He took a drink, wiped his forehead with the back of his hand. Julia leant against the door, feeling the cold wood with her fingers. Swinton stood upright.

'I met her in town. Quite an accident, a few days ago. I made a date with her for yesterday evening to meet her in the Red Lion for a drink at half-past eight. I never thought she'd turn up.'

The voice, the story, everything was far away and could have, Julia thought, nothing to do with them.

'Funnily enough she did turn up. We had quite a few Martinis, and then I brought her back here to the launch. I gathered she was fed up about something. Some man had told her he couldn't meet her again.'

'I had told her that.'

It was Swinton, the man Julia knew and recognized; it was only what he said that seemed to have no meaning.

'She was cut up about it, yet being cut up made

her gay, almost hysterical. She was funny, you know. She'd make you laugh all the time, and yet it was a bit frightening as if there was no telling what she'd do next.

'We got on to whisky on board and kept that up for some time. Then she asked me to take her back to her place where she had some records she wanted us to dance to.

'Naturally, I did. Though it was a job steering the old ship after all we'd put on board.'

He looked up at them trying to laugh. Their faces were turned towards her, both unsmiling.

'Anyway, I got her home and we lit the lamp and started up the gramophone. She had a bottle of gin and we got back on to that after the whisky.'

This, she supposed, was what was involved in finding things out. Listening to the story Julia felt, however, no wiser, only farther away from the truth than when she had stood, that afternoon, in the dazzling sun-soaked room.

'We danced together for a time and she seemed quite happy. Tell you the truth, I was getting a bit on, you know. I can't remember the rest all that clearly.'

He looked up at Swinton hopefully, but Swinton said nothing.

'Then, suddenly, she began to turn on me. She was like an animal. Look, she did that.'

He rolled up his sleeve and Julia saw the long marks of scratches on his arm. She realized that, for some reason, the man was sorry for himself, feeling, in some obscure way, wronged.

'What was it all about?'

'Take it easy now. Julia's here.'

'Just tell us.'

'Well, if you must have it . . . Tell you it was a bit difficult to get it clear what she was talking about.'

'Try anyway.'

'As I told you, Swinton, I knew her a long time ago. We got on together and – well, you know the rest. I didn't see her for a long time after that . . .'

The extraordinary thing, Julia realized, is that, although he's frightened, he's pleased that this has happened to him, he feels that it's important.

'Apparently, or so she told me last night, she'd had some trouble as the result of it, been in the family way as far as I could make out. It had all led to a quarrel with her brother. Look, the gramophone was going, we'd about finished her bottle of gin, it was difficult to understand . . .'

Difficult? Julia thought, it's impossible, only this, no doubt, is the simplest part of it.

'Anyway, it seemed she blamed all her troubles on me, everything that had happened from then on. She was excited, not herself at all. I tell you, she attacked me. She was quite frail, you know; brittle, I suppose that's what you'd call her. But she was going then like a whirlwind.'

'And so you –?'

'I retreated, old man. Up the stairs. You know, I told her to hold on, have a heart, not to be damn silly. She took no notice. She came up at me. I didn't even touch her. She was kicking out at me and she stumbled on the stairs and fell. That's what happened. That's all. I swear it. I'll swear that anywhere.'

His hands were over his face, his shoulders quivered. It may be that this is the end, Julia thought, the final, ultimate truth, and that's why it looks so unreal and unconvincing.

'That's all right. Have a drink now.'

'Thanks.' He looked up, a fat man with his glasses off, his eyes full of tears. Julia pressed herself away from him against the wood.

Campbell turned to Swinton. 'What are you going to do?'

'Nothing now. I'm going to make a statement to the police tomorrow. You'll have to make one too. I don't see why they shouldn't believe you.'

'Why should I go to the police? There's nothing to connect me with her. Nothing at all.'

He was looking round the cabin as if, Julia thought, for a way of escape.

Swinton said: 'There'll be my statement. And the photograph I found here.'

'You took that?'

Swinton nodded.

Campbell sighed. 'Poor old Mol. She didn't mean to half the time, but she always made trouble. Too attractive and too damned unstable, I suppose.' He looked at Swinton hopefully. 'It may be all right.'

'It may be.'

'Will I have to tell them about what happened all that time ago?'

'It's up to you. We'll leave you now.'

'Oh, now, look, you two. Don't go away. Stay a little while. Just one for the road.'

Julia heard an awful, beseeching voice, and heard the fear and the loneliness in it.

'I can't help thinking of her. She lay so still and all the wrong shape. It only took a minute. Imagine.' He looked at them with bewilderment. 'All that time ago, for all I know she might have had the child.'

Julia heard herself speaking for the first time. 'I don't think so,' she said.

'Julia. Be a good girl. Stay for one more.'

The walls of the cabin seemed to press down on her, the sound of his voice was everywhere.

'Or let me come with you. Only for a little while. You missed the party.'

Julia seemed to have to fight to get to the door. Then she ran up the steps and heard Swinton behind her. She was out in the rain, breathing the cold air, feeling the water against her cheek. She was back in the darkness she could understand.

Julia and Swinton were back in the garden. They could hear Campbell calling after them from the boat.

'I've told you what you wanted, haven't I? Don't leave me now. You've got all you want.'

She heard Swinton shout back: 'We must go. I must go with Julia.'

'All right, the hell with you. I'm going up to

the pub. I'll collect some people. You can join us later. I'm taking the boat up to the pub. Not past that bloody island. I'll get lots of people. A whole party. Come on later.'

Wild and anxious, calling in the darkness, his voice might have been the voice of a thin man.

They heard the engines cough and start and then the launch bumped against the bank. The water churned, the lights of the boat drew away. They were left alone.

'JULIA.'

They were in the dark, blind after the bright cabin. They couldn't see each other. She felt his hand on her arm and shook it off.

'Leave me alone.'

'What's the matter?'

She didn't want to go back to the house, to be with him. She ran into the darkness from which, as the dazzling light of the cabin died out of her eyes, grew trees, bushes, beds of pale ghostly flowers. The rain was stopping and the air was only a little wet. She heard him shouting behind her.

'Julia, I had to show you, I didn't kill her.'

'What's it matter?'

She came to the boathouse, on it St Anthony in pious benediction blessed the souls of the drowning: white in the shadows about her, she saw his plaster foot. For the second time in the day she wrenched open the door.

'I thought you were thinking . . .' Swinton followed her in. She saw a floor of water with a concrete platform round it; a pile of sacks on which he might still be sleeping. She stood looking at them in the darkness, trying to find a shape that could be a man.

'I had to let you hear . . .' He was speaking to her again.

There was no one. Nothing but the sacks and the shadows. She put her hands over her eyes, again she moved away when he tried to touch her.

'It's all over now.' His voice was tired and quiet.

She opened her hands, saw him sitting on a box lighting a cigarette. She threw back her arms and let the words tumble out, echoing against the damp walls.

'It's been a bad day but that was the worst. Solemnly to drag me in there to listen to that story. So seriously you took it and now you think it's all over. Just because that fat bastard told us how she fell downstairs. What does it matter to me? I'm only your wife.'

'Is it because I went there at all?'

Swinton looked up, frowning, bewildered. He had never seen Julia do this before and the thought that he might, for all she cared, have been a murderer, alarmed and impressed him.

'I went to get that stupid case. I swam to get it because I was afraid of the police, not for you, for the children. I don't mind what you did.'

'If I'd killed her . . .'

'I wouldn't have cared . . .' She saw him holding the cigarette between his fingers with the imperturbability of a night watchman sitting by his brazier. For nearly a whole day, for the first time for fifteen years, she had been out of love with him.

'I don't mind. I don't mind, I tell you.'

'Look, Julia. I met her on the train . . .'

Swinton knew he would have to explain but he couldn't find words; the language of the emotions was dead to him, dead as the Latin he had forgotten since he was at school. After the peace, the growing old, the monosyllables at breakfast, he had to sit in a dark boathouse in the middle of the night and try to remember the old words again.

'It was all unimportant. It's all over.'

It wasn't unimportant, it was vital, urgent, insoluble. She saw him trying to remember the words which would discover it all and her anger left her, turning to a terrible friendliness. She sat down beside him, staring at the dirty water under their feet. It was always possible that, sometime in the night, the man would return.

'I met her on the train. A couple of weeks ago.'

Julia knew she had to listen but her thoughts strayed to the man who had come so casually and fatally into her day. Thinking of him and looking into the shadows around her, she began in a glimmering, half-conscious way, to have an idea of what had happened. If she and her husband had both, in their different ways, been reaching out for something outside each other, if they had both suddenly been drawn to a different, young and cruel world in which they no longer had any place, couldn't the day possibly be explained? She was too tired, too preoccupied with her own sudden loneliness to explain it. But the man, if he had been there, would have given them an explanation. Or he'd have confounded them all with a question.

She said: 'Were you so tired of us?'

He shook his head slowly.

'Not tired of you at all. It happened almost by accident. We got talking. She asked me to come in one evening for a drink.'

Julia was frightened, above all, of being able to sympathize with him, of being able to understand how he felt. When she could do that, she thought, their lives together would be over. She wanted to be angry. She said:

'Was she as beautiful as they all say?'

'She was strange. It was difficult not to look at her.'

'Let me see her photograph. You told Campbell you had it.'

'I threw it away. It wasn't true when I told him I still had it.'

She looked at him curiously, wondering how often, recently, he had lied.

Julia said: 'How often did you go?'

'Three or four times, I forget.'

'Why did you want to go?'

'I thought, in a little while I am going to be old. Something like that. I don't know.'

And I, too, Julia thought, am hovering on the brink of age. In time, people who found Susan beautiful, would say, her mother too, she must have been a lovely woman in her day.

'That brother I told you about,' Julia said. 'He came and talked. Everything he said was so extraordinary. He was like no one I'd ever met before. He made me feel . . . that I was only just beginning. He was here nearly all day. I never even shook hands with him. We never touched each other.'

'Did you want to?'

'Naturally I did.'

That might have made them equal, but it still made it impossible for them to be in love.

'So you went round for a drink?' Julia went on. The man, she remembered, had told her that she couldn't stop finding things out.

'Yes.'

'And never told me.'

'No.'

Swinton remembered. It was no use, neither Julia's questions nor his answers could ever explain it. No words he had ever learnt or would ever discover could explain what he had felt when he went there. Only the look of it came back to him. The room was so brilliant and chaotic, with nothing that seemed of any use except the bed, surely too large for anyone living on their own. And he saw the girl, young enough to be his child but, as the young are, older than the generation before her, more knowledgeable, more intent on destruction than he could ever be. He could see it but already it was blurred, out of focus, dimmed by the passing of so little time.

'It's over, Julia. It never really started. We'll forget it all soon.'

'Will we forget today?'

The rain had stopped. Outside them and above the boathouse clouds drifted away and the night was clear with a moon which began to flood the house and garden, picking out the sharp leaves of the tree on the lawn. The river outside lightened, became silver and there was a pale reflected light on the boathouse itself. Julia and Swinton sat side by side, divided from each other by an enormous loneliness.

Soon they would go back to the house. In the morning the children would get up early and they would be caught up again in the automatic, necessary activity of another day. Sam would want his breakfast and there was no time, when they woke up, to sleep or make love. In the houseboat, Swinton thought, time had been childless, unurgent. There, the only thing of importance had been the moment of excitement, the destruction which must follow had seemed distant and unimportant. He remembered sitting on the edge of the girl's bed, finding her a cigarette, seeing how you could destroy all the years of your life as you might, at a touch, let off a bomb which could destroy a city, and perhaps, by doing that, start life again.

'Did you go to bed with her?'

'No.'

The question and answer were formal, automatic and meaningless. Julia thought, we're not getting anywhere, we may as well stop talking.

'I saw the room,' she said. 'I can see the point.'

'Yes. You went there.'

Suddenly he took off his coat and put it round her. They neither of them knew what it was they had to say, what truth or which lie was necessary to bring them together again.

Julia said: 'Would it have gone on? If she was still . . . if nothing had happened?'

'I ended it when I went there last.'

'When was that?'

'Last night. I walked that way down the river before I came home. I couldn't help going over.'

'What was wrong with coming home?'

He frowned, remembering.

'I thought of how it had been in the morning. The children sitting round and you drinking your coffee standing up. All those names on the cups.'

She looked at him, peering at his face in amazement through the darkness. For the first time something he had said had led to a discovery.

'You don't like the names on the cups?'

'Often, for no reason, I've wanted to smash the bloody things.'

She laughed, uncontrollably, alarming him still more. It was almost, she thought, as if she might get on with this man, if only she knew who he was.

'At breakfast,' she said, 'the thing I can't stand is the way you read out the advertisements.'

He looked back at her, curious, feeling startled and oddly younger.

'It must have been last night you left your case.'

'I expect so. I only stayed five minutes.'

He had gone, had he, to make sure he would never go again?

'Did you make love then?'

'No.'

She wondered if, like her, he was regretting it.

And then she became frightened of the darkness and the water, remembering that the girl was dead.

He remembered that she was dead and knew that, before she died, she must have hated him.

The evening before the girl had put the bottles and the glasses on the table by the bed and said that she was sorry, not knowing that he was coming, that there were no rose petals. He had told her that he couldn't stay and she had said he was a difficult man, but he had a difficult life and it must be dreary beyond belief, surely his wife, by this time, must have got used to things like this; if she hadn't she was far too possessive. He had known that she didn't understand it and he had told her it wasn't difficult, his life, on the contrary, it was easy; it was its easiness that made him want to complicate it. And then she had told him that she knew he wasn't going to come again. So, after he left, she had gone out with Campbell.

It was the thing no one had the right to do, to

experiment with the life they didn't mean to live out to the end. He had done it and he was nowhere, in the dark boathouse, alone.

'I told her I wouldn't come again.'

'So that was the end. All the time you had.'

'Yes.'

'And I only had today.'

They were both gone, the brother and the sister, and Julia and Swinton, more near to each other and more remote than any brother and sister, were left to manage as best they could.

Julia said: 'What now?'

'Surely there's no alternative.'

'No alternative to what we do; but to what we think about what we do?'

'Just the same, surely?'

She sat beside him, her hands under her thighs for warmth, looking at the water.

'Never the same, never the same again. Don't you see that?'

'Julia, I'm sorry . . .'

'Don't be. There's no point. It may all be better, different, anyhow.' They seemed to have been talking a long time, the anger and the strange friendliness had gone, but they were sitting close together. The day had finished, carried them away from their home and their children, into the last, solitary hours of the night.

'There was so much,' she said, 'we took for granted.'

'But it was still there, when we needed it.'

And now, she wondered, shall we live the rest

of our lives and never see this opening, this distant vista of an outside world again? She was silent a long time.

'What's the matter?'

'It's terrible. That she's dead.'

In the end they went to bed. The house was silent and they walked through it without speaking, far from each other. They undressed in silence and Swinton looked out on the clear, moonlit garden as he opened the window. He said:

'Tomorrow's Saturday. I thought of taking the children out on the river. I hope it'll be fine.'

Looking up Julia saw the moon, the little grey clouds moving away from it, the top of the tree.

'It's going to be all right.'

'Good,' he said.

He got into the bed beside her and they lay still, unrelaxed, not touching. In such a way the Norman knight and his wife lay on the tomb in the town church, their feet pointed, their hands crossed. They were both cold.

It was over, a day finished which they had thought endless, lived through before they had time to understand it. Outside their bed, the house, the garden, the river itself, were all quiet. The other people they had seen might never have existed. They turned their heads on the pillow, only seeing each other. They saw in their faces something new, which they could not yet recognize, which they would have to grow used to in the days to come.

THE moon faded, became small and white and
the large, pallid sun thickened the mist over the
river. The mist rolled like smoke, hiding the
swans and the moored boats and the trunks of the
willow trees. Daylight coldly entered the children's bedrooms.

Susan looked out at it. She hadn't heard them
coming to bed and she wondered if they were still
talking. She wondered what they could possibly
have to say to each other. They were obviously
bored and yet they wanted to be alone, to go out
alone together and to be alone in their bedroom.
It seemed stupid to her; how rightly, at school,
they had all decided not to marry.

Sam looked out into the room, watching the
furniture gradually return to its accustomed
places, restored by the reassuring light of day.
Today he would make his father buy him a blazer
with gold buttons and a megaphone. He would
cycle along the towpath and shout instructions to
Tom who, pulling on the oars, would drive his

skiff through the water at record speed. He would buy a stopwatch. He would become the youngest trainer on the river. He was the youngest trainer on the river, carried shoulder-high with Tom by the crowd, on the last day of the regatta. In his arms he had an enormous silver cup. Round him caps and straw hats rose into the air. Over the river the fireworks started. Tom picked out in his skiff in lights, rockets moving like squirrels up into the dark branches of the sky, exploding with blue, green and golden stars. Up the rockets went, always brighter and higher, the scarlet balls of fire floated down on parachutes, the dead rockets' sticks fell among the band and everyone laughed. The catherine wheels started, shedding fire on to the water as they whistled round. A group of men, the band leader in the scarlet uniform, the mayor in his fur hat, stood round Tom. How did you do it? I didn't do it, my trainer did it for me. The fireworks were over. The day had almost started. Sam blinked and shook the sleep out of his head. He knew he was only pretending, he knew, now he thought about it, that his friend was too old ever to race a boat again.

Tom opened his eyes as wide as he could and looked round the dark bedroom. He could still see the big brass knobs on his bed, his trousers over the back of a chair, the pale china basin and water-jug, the frame of the religious picture over the door. He was alive. It was only if he shut his eyes and went to sleep that he was afraid it might take him, send him spinning down some dark and

sickly switchback as happened when he closed his
eyes on going to bed drunk. And yet, he was tired
and longed for sleep. He lay still, knowing he
wasn't right, wondering what could be wrong
with him. He was as weak, he thought, as a
bloody chicken, and he wondered if he'd live to
have another woman. Probably not, women
didn't grow on trees, not the sort he liked, the
sort he could get too, when he had his health.
There were times, on summer evenings by the
lock, when they came to him like flies to meat.
There was something to be thankful for and that
was that he had a parcel of pound notes saved
up under the bed and another in the back of the
wardrobe. Never been bothered with any children so who was to have it? If he died he'd have
to leave it to the Holy Father like his wife had told
him. Let him live another day and he could spend
his money, cheat the Holy Father. He could invest
it in brandy and drink himself back to life. He
pushed his back into the bed as if he were opening
the gates of his lock. He pushed as hard as he
could, pushing away from the dark shadows
around him. It was a miracle. He was going to
live another day.

The grey sponge of a sun slowly wiped the mist
from the river, leaving it clear as a looking-glass.
The swans appeared, moving in families, leaving
a long wake of black and silver ripples. The water
moved slowly, endlessly, towards the lock to
tumble, yellow and angry, into the pool of the
river. With it floated driftwood and torn-out

weeds, a plank from a derelict houseboat, an empty bottle, a discarded cigarette carton and somewhere, out in the middle of the river, the curling, sinking, half-submerged photograph of a girl.